BAT AND THE JACK

FURRY UNITED COALITION NEWBIE ACADEMY

A. GREGORY

ACKNOWLEDGMENTS

Mr. Fire, you wonderful beast, you. Thanks for being my rock, my partner, my biggest supporter. I love you with all of my little black heart, and I will forever and ever.

A huge thanks to Eve for letting me play in her awesome world again and for letting me be my weird self.

Another huge thanks goes to Jessica Ripley who is quite literally one of the best humans in this world. You're an amazing friend, and I am very lucky to have you in my life.

To Devin Govaere, thanks for making my book baby all clean. You're the best!

And of course, a huge thank you goes to you, dear reader. I hope you enjoyed Vera and Jack's story.

For Mr. Fire,

1

VERA

This is it.

This is my big moment.

In a few seconds, I won't just have a diploma but a *badge*. I will no longer be Vera Slaski, failed attorney. I'll be *Agent Slaski*.

My palms are a sweaty mess, marring the smooth line of my petal pink skirt every time I flatten it, but I don't care. For once, I don't mind a less-than-perfect attire.

Agent Slaski doesn't care if she's flawless.

She cares about law, justice, and locking up bad guys.

I am a bat. Hear me echolocate.

The small room isn't exactly packed, but there are enough people here to witness my triumph. My parents, who flew in from Toronto, beam at me with pride. They are physically incapable of *not* being proud of me. That's sweet, really. But it also has a price: soul-crushing pressure to make sure that I deserve their praise.

I could quit everything, join a circus, and I'm pretty sure Mom and Dad would still cheer me on.

Beside me, my little sister, Raya, drums her fingers on

her distressed jeans. Thin white veins of material, unweaving themselves in protest, stretch against her bent knee. It's seconds away from tearing from an almost-hole to a full one.

Not that Raya would mind if her holey denim broke out with more tears. She doesn't care about anything much. Pissing me off? Now, there is something she excels at with very little effort. Were it an Olympic sport, she'd be the undisputed champ.

When I invited Raya to the ceremony, I specifically requested that she wear something appropriate for the occasion's gravitas.

Raya rolled her eyes and scoffed when I chided her for her attire earlier. A pair of pale blue jeans one chromosome away from being a rag, a white ribbed tank, and combat boots don't scream *Congratulations, graduate.*

People *say* we look alike, but it's a sisterly optical illusion. Where my brown hair is always coiffed into an immaculate elongated bob, Raya lets her waves run wild. Even in the dead of a Canadian winter, she could pass for Queen Beach Bum—nonchalant and unruffled. I'm all about order, while Raya will disorganize her life simply to stress me out.

Sort of like how she dropped out of university to join up with FUCN'A—the Furry United Coalition Newbie Academy—a few weeks after me.

I was *livid*, but today isn't about her or the leather jacket I begged her to ditch before the ceremony began.

This is about me *finally* attaining my goal. I will *finally* be able to make a difference in this world.

My cousin and a FUC forensic anthropologist, Mila Starling, gives me a thumbs-up from across the aisle. Her husband, FUC agent T-Bone Thrussel, gives me an encouraging head nod. They understand what this means to me. Their presence here is heartwarming and emboldening.

Alyce Cooper, director of FUCN'A and all-around badass, rattles off the names of a few other newly minted agents before she calls *my* name.

My heart climbs into my throat as I leap to my feet.

This is it.

I'm getting my FUC badge.

This moment is made all the more amazing because my personal hero, Chase Brownsmith, is here with his wife, Miranda. Mila pulled about a thousand strings to get him here so I could meet him. It's awesome and terrifying all at once. Chase Brownsmith is a legend, and I've based my future on his path. He might be a bear, but I'm positive that I can follow in his paw prints—even if I have to fly overhead.

Chase used to be a lawyer, but the bear joined the ranks of FUC after a series of events that included becoming the target of an evil scientist's scheme, getting kidnapped, being rescued by FUC's sabre tooth bunny, and falling in love with said bunny. He's an inspiration to me. I really thought I could change the world when I became a lawyer. *Wrong.* So damn wrong. I couldn't exactly pick and choose my clients, even if I wanted to.

Let's be real.

There's only a certain amount of mental gymnastics I can do to convince myself that the big, burly man with the rap sheet as long as my two arms combined is *innocent*.

Lawyers don't only protect the innocent.

Sometimes, we have to defend the bad guys.

I didn't like it. At all.

I wanted to be the kind of lawyer who helped people, but I managed to defend crooks and villains in my short career. How was I supposed to live with myself?

I couldn't.

When my older cousin Mila joined FUC, she told me all about Chase Brownsmith. That led me right here. Standing in front of my family and peers and Director Cooper. My life will definitely change forever.

"Come on, Vera." Director Cooper waves me forward like this isn't the most significant few seconds of my life.

Do not fall flat on your face, Vera.

She holds out her hand for me to shake while grabbing a rolled-up sheet of paper. She passes it to me, and my trembling fingers stretch out to take it. It's significant. Monumental. It's not just reaching out for my diploma; it's starting a whole new life.

In my excitement, I zealously grab the diploma and tug.

The sickening *swish* of paper slicing through skin rattles in my brain. Director Cooper winces as a string of blood pebbles along her finger. She wiggles her hand before bringing her injured digit to her mouth to staunch the bleeding.

The most amazing moment of my life is ruined.

I *know* it. I *feel* it.

Do. Not. Pass. Out.

I look away, my stomach rolling with acid. The floor lurches under me, and I reach out to steady myself on the wooden podium. And that's when I see it. The drop of blood on my pale pink skirt.

Flapping membrane.

I grip the pulpit and force deep gulps of air into my lungs. The edge of my vision blurs.

I should've had some blood last night.

On shaky legs, I turn away from Director Cooper. Mom and Dad watch me, expectant and worried. Raya, cocky and annoying, crosses her arms. She *knows* why I'm fighting to stay conscious.

Then there's Chase Brownsmith, lawyer turned agent, standing there looking as perplexed as a vampire bat trying to drink from an iron bull. He frowns, no doubt confused by the sudden stop to the ceremony.

I really should've drank some blood last night.

That's my last conscious thought before my eyes roll back and I fall into the dark.

⸻

"Oh, no-no-no. Did she pass out?"

"Sure looks like it."

"Is she okay?"

"This happens sometimes," Mom sighs.

Wait.

Why is my mother here? Where is *here*? Why does my head hurt?

Slowly, I crack one eye open. Above me, the ceiling shimmies and undulates. A few people stand, gawking down; frowns and smiles melt together in the perfect puddle of embarrassment.

"You okay?" Chase asks.

"I've got some carrot cake here." Miranda shoves an overfull container crammed with a piece of cake about the size of a small child toward me.

"It's hardly the time," Chase explains to his wife, grabbing the dish. "She's lost consciousness." He flips the lid open, grabs the cake, and bites into it, leaving merely crumbs behind. If I wasn't about to hurl, I'd be impressed with his eating skill.

Miranda clicks her tongue. "Hence the cake, Chase. It'll

level off her blood sugar. Or it would have before you ate it all."

"I really don't think that blood *sugar* is the problem here," Raya taunts.

How my own sister—my flesh and blood—can look so pleased right now is proof alone that I've messed up.

"What in the name of FUC happened?" Director Cooper pipes up, tapping her foot. "Why is one of my future agents in a dead swoon? What is this? A salon for temperamental ladies? Up, Vera. On your feet."

"Yes, Director."

Only problem is, my knees have stopped being knees. Oh, they're still there. My kneecaps are intact, and by rights, I should be able to stand on my own two feet—if my legs weren't suddenly made of jiggling gelatin. The floor *needs* to stop moving before I even *try* to stand.

The smell of blood lingers in the air, the sharp metallic scent prickling my nose with the promise of more fainting.

Pull yourself together, Vera.

"Well?" my future boss snaps. She's not merely tapping her foot; she's ready to break out into a full jig.

Chase takes hold of my hands and hoists me up. I am nothing but a collapsed rag doll in my hero's arms.

Kill. Me. Now.

It took me all of two seconds to fail at being an agent.

"Here we are." The bear shifter helps me into one of the chairs and pats my shoulder like a clumsy uncle who doesn't know how to console his niece. "You okay?"

I nod because what the hell else am I going to do? Admit to a room full of people that I am a vampire bat who passes out at the sight of blood?

I can't.

That would be the fastest way of losing my position as a FUC agent before I even get my hands on my badge.

"Someone really needs to explain to me what's happened," Director Cooper grumbles. "Nolan is on his way to check you out, Vera."

"That's not necessary," I say. Rather, I plead. "I'm fine."

Director Cooper wags her still-bleeding finger at me. "Don't tell lies, Vera. I can sniff 'em out from a mile away."

My ass melts into the chair, and I really long to disappear. Actually, if I'm wishing for things, it would be the ability to not faint every time I see blood. That's what I really need.

"My office," Director Cooper commands before turning on her heels and leaving the room.

Mom sits beside me and drapes her arms around my shoulder. "Are you okay, Moppet?"

I wince at the nickname I've hated since the day it was bestowed on me on my fourth birthday when the clown got a nosebleed. Other kids pass out because clowns are scary as hell and have no business being at a kid's party.

Me? I nosedived into my cake because the man bled.

Dad sighs. I can *feel* his shame and disappointment. "I thought you were over all that."

"She's over it all right," Raya quips. "Looks like I'll lap you." She grins, shrugs, and saunters out.

Not a chance in hell am I going to let Raya get her badge before me.

2

———

NORBERT

Every time I hear *whistleblower*, my mind fills with the image of a crossing guard. A living, breathing statue stuck in the middle of a busy intersection, wearing an ugly reflective orange vest, hands out to stop traffic and blowing like mad into a bright yellow kazoo.

Cars and trucks perpetually rush by with no concern for the rules or basic human decency.

There the guard stands, honking his kazoo, knowing that, at any second, he could be killed.

That he *will* be killed.

That's me right now.

I'm not using a whistle but my mouth, and I have to admit some pretty horrible things.

The cars are rich and powerful shifters, and the only thing standing between me and certain death is my contact with the Cryptozoian Council.

I miss the simplicity of my farm life.

This is my own damn fault. I got myself into this mess because—just like Icarus—I wanted to fly too close to the sun.

Shoulda stuck to your plants, dude. People suck.

A faded green ball cap is smashed down on my head to hide my easily recognizable tight black curls. The visor knocks against my glasses every time I look around the room. I'm two seconds away from being discovered. I can almost *feel* the walls closing in around me.

I thought meeting in a busy coffee shop would be a good idea. I even picked a town away from my farm. No one *should* be capable of following me back to my place, but that's a problem for Future Me.

First, I have to survive this meeting—*if* my contact actually shows up.

She better be here soon because one of the teenagers buying overly sweet iced drinks is seconds away from taking one gander at me and screaming *Unabomber.*

That'll be the end of that.

I tug on my hat, cross my arms, and scan the coffee shop once again. The pack of teens gathered at the counter shriek and shrill like ordering a coffee is the new mating call.

I miss the quiet of my gardens.

Plants don't talk. Not exactly anyway. Their language is way more subtle, something I appreciate.

It would be way easier if I knew *who* I was expecting.

Val Downer, the agent I'm meeting, gave me no description of herself. All I know is that I was to come into this café, order two coffees, and wait until she made her appearance.

Did I watch one too many spy movies in preparation for this? Maybe.

Not that it helped. My paranoia is ratcheted up to a million. If she isn't here in the next two minutes, I'll leave.

Pfft. Who am I kidding?

I can't go. I'm stuck here, and I'm stuck in my own damn life.

The door swings open, and a petite woman with long black hair braided back from her face walks in with a laptop bag and one serious glower. Without warning or preamble, she grabs the chair at my small round table and plops into it.

"I'm saving that seat," I grumble. "Waiting on someone."

"You don't say," she snaps back, producing a compact computer from her black bag. It sings its way into life before she begins typing furiously at it.

It's on the tip of my tongue to ask her if she is Agent Downer, but it's not like I'm used to this.

Hell, the last time I left my house was six months ago. I hated every second of my time away from my cabin and farm. When I got back, more than a few of my precious crops were dead. No doubt, it was their protest at my absence.

The same would happen again.

If my fennel and Brussels sprout kick the bucket while I'm here, I'll be *seriously* pissed off. I wasn't leaving again for a decade. That was a damn promise.

"Look..." I inject all of my macho manliness into my tone, pitching my voice low. "I really am waiting on someone. If you'd kindly—"

"Don't get excited, Norbert." She rolls her eyes and spins the laptop toward me. The webpage for Vitality stares back at me.

"Oh," I mumble. "So it's you. You're Val Dormer."

She nods. "Did you bring the files?"

It's my turn to give a surreptitious bow of the head, only *slightly* panicked that I might have given myself away to my enemies. "How do I know you're who you say you are?"

She arches a brow, seconds away from scowling. "I don't have time for this."

"And I don't have time to die." Not my best line, but it

does the trick.

Downer produces a badge, and on the sly, she flips it toward me. "I'm a koala shifter. Satisfied?"

I slide a small flash drive onto the table. Agent Dormer scoffs at the bright butternut squash-shaped memory stick.

What was she expecting? I'm a botanist. A subsistence farmer to boot. Obviously, I've got a passion for veg.

"It's all here?" She slides the squash into her computer and begins typing away furiously.

"Everything I could get," I correct.

Her brow furrows. "Norbert, if we don't have everything we need in this, our deal is off."

My hands fist on the tabletop. "No way. They'll kill me if they find out I have these files. You *swore* you'd give me protection."

She has the nerve to wave me off. "If the Cryptozoian Council and our FUCN'A go-between, Erhart Knop, don't have enough, neither organization can continue the investigation. And without a proper case, we can't put the company on trial."

"Everything you need is in there," I promise. "Now, you guaranteed that your people could keep me safe. That you'd stop the toxic waste dumping. I've held up my end of the bargain."

Downer makes a noncommittal sound, and I wonder what kind of disposition koala shifters have. Could she dispatch me in two seconds flat with a well-aimed blow, or would she have to be a bit more creative about it?

"We're good?" I repeat, ready to leave and move on with my simple life.

I'm never, ever getting involved with a human again.

Val narrows her keen eyes, a small pucker drawing her brows together. "You're hiding something."

Somethings. S. Plural.

My shoulders tense, but I try to wave her off. "What?" I cough. "No." I fake-sneeze. "Not in the least." I grab my cup of coffee, toying with the sleeve. *What a waste of natural resources.*

"Norbert," she warns. "What aren't you telling me?"

"Why would you ask that?"

She doesn't know. She can't. It's impossible. Be cool, Norbert. Be cool as dirt in the spring.

"You're twitchy." Val crosses her arms, continuing her staredown. "If we can't rely on you, you'll be removed to a secret and undisclosed location."

"I'm not hiding anything," I lie. Might as well be a cucumber growing in the garden for all the lying around I'm doing *right* to Val Downer's face.

"Fine. If you say so. We'll figure it out if you are, you know. We're sending a FUC agent to keep watch over you. They're going to stay here with you until you testify for the Cryptozoian Council. Keep you safe."

I snort. "Sure. Keep me safe from Lisbeth Bannon."

"She's not all-powerful."

"She's trying to be," I shoot back.

Downer nods. "Hopefully, this will be the first step to stopping her."

And just like that, as fast as she arrived, Agent Downer is gone. She leaves no more information about my protection or the next step. My gut churns with panic. This might've been a grievous mistake.

But it's too late now.

I can't put the knowledge back into its hiding spot like I can't undo the experiments.

All I *can* do is go back to my farm and hope I'm around for harvest.

3

VERA

I'm a broken bat.

Not a piece of wood dudes use to hurl balls at each other. Nope. A flying, blood-sucking vampire bat. Itty bitty with a biological need to drink a bit of blood every single day to survive.

I'm broken because I am *terrified* of blood.

The mere sight of it makes me queasy. I can't stomach it. It's a damn miracle that I can live with so very little of it. It's even more of a wonder that I managed to complete my training at the Furry United Coalition Newbie Academy without falling in a dead faint.

Every time someone got hurt, I teetered on the edge of discovery.

Maybe it would've been better if someone had called me out on it before yesterday.

I didn't get my badge.

I got *grounded*.

Director Cooper might as well have stamped *Cadet* on my forehead in permanent marker. I am not allowed to graduate or go on missions until I can prove to her that I can be around vast quantities of blood without passing out.

Vast quantities.

Those were the exact words she used once Nolan was done checking me over.

Every single person I walked past today gave me the side-eye. I could *hear* their pity and scorn.

I wanted to spend the day in my dorm room, feeling sorry for myself, but Mila and T-Bone stopped by and basically forced me to have lunch with them.

At least they keep nocturnal hours like me, which means that the cafeteria wasn't packed. I settled at one of the tables, too emotional to eat anything. My cousin and her dashing husband grabbed food, bickering like an old married couple despite the fact they haven't been paired up for all that long.

They met on a mission, fell in love, got engaged after six months, and before Mila could walk down the aisle in a black tutu like she wanted to, she was pregnant.

And to think their love story never would have happened if Sveta Markov hadn't escaped from prison. The notorious mass murderer known as the Bloody Doctor is my aunt and Mila's mom. The former hematologist is obsessed with blood. It turned into full-blown mania that led her down some dark and seriously twisted paths.

The Bloody Doctor is *all* about the blood.

Apparently, I'm the only vampire bat who can't cope with blood.

It's not one of those ironic situations.

I had an aversion to blood *way* before Aunt Sveta was caught. The long—disgusting—list of her crimes didn't exactly turn me on to blood. She loves it too much, and I love it none. A balance, life is not.

"Stop moping," Mila instructs with her teacher's voice. My hugely pregnant cousin is clad all in black, her T-shirt, which reads, *I grow bones* with a baby skeleton, stretched over her baby bump. She rubs at it with a wince of pain. She's about to pop but refuses to go on maternity leave. There is every chance she'll go into labor in her creepy basement office, surrounded by bones.

"This is for you, Vera," She shoves a plateful of steak tartar right under my nose. "Compliments of our dear director."

My stomach rolls with bile. My hand flies to my mouth as I screw my eyes shut. "Nope." The mound of raw ground beef oozes blood onto the white plate. The tuft of green garnish is downright comical. As if *that* makes the dish palatable.

"Come *on*," Mila scolds. "It's not that bad. It's actually delicious. You need it to survive."

"I don't see how." I turn my head away, thankful for my lip gloss. The happy aroma of cotton candy wafting up from my lips saves me from passing out. *Again.*

Mila clicks her tongue and digs into the tartar with gusto. "You know Alyce won't let you go on your first assignment until you get some blood down your gullet." She points a bloody fork at me. "No hurling."

"Leave the poor woman alone, Mila." T-Bone settles into the seat beside her, his hand instinctively going to her stomach. She slaps it away.

"Hands to yourself, beefcakes, or I'll make a meal out of you."

T-Bone beams at her with cow eyes, full of love and adoration. "You're so motherly. It gives me so much joy to know how caring you'll be for our little one."

Mila scowls at him. "I better be growing a bat. If I gotta

push out an enormous Hairy Coo, I'm never speaking to you again."

He kisses her cheek before tearing into his massive sandwich.

Undeterred by her potential calving, Mila nudges the rest of the steak tartar toward me. "T's had some before, and he enjoys it. Give it a try."

Until that second, I didn't know it was possible to feel like a color, but I am definitely the color green. Not envy. Nope. Green like cartoons before they blow chunks.

This week has turned into a nightmare. I peek down at my clothes to make sure I'm not naked. I'm not entirely convinced I'm clothed with the way things keep going from bad to worse.

I'm fully dressed, and this isn't a night terror.

It's real life.

Damn.

I *almost* had my diploma in hand. My whole destiny hinged on a papercut, and *voila*. Just like that, all my plans vanished.

You don't know what shame is until you pass out in front of your peers and own personal hero.

Now *everyone* knows I'm the vampire bat with an aversion to blood. The shame!

Oh. And Director Cooper is keeping me grounded and as a cadet until I manage to drink some blood. I don't think it's fair to add a condition to my training this late in the game, but Alyce Cooper can do whatever she wants. She's the boss.

"Maybe I'll just go back to practicing law." I don't mean it, but I've got no clue how to get past this. I am forever doomed as a cadet. Raya will lap me and wave her badge in my face every chance she gets.

Mila shakes her head in response, her firetruck red hair flying everywhere. "Not a chance. This is way too important." She pushes the plate closer to me. "First step tartar, second step blood."

"Stop," I plead.

"You're giving us a bad name," Mila quips.

I snort out a laugh. As the resident forensic anthropologist with a penchant for listening to death metal while talking to the bones of murder victims, Mila isn't exactly the picture of a well-adjusted adult. She is married to a cattle shifter: the very same animal vampire bats are known to prey on. Not to mention her addiction to inappropriate shirts. I love my cousin, but last week, she taught a class while wearing a tee that read, *Will Work For A Bone.*

That makes us eccentric. Not my aversion to blood.

It doesn't *really* give us a bad name. On the contrary, the cadets actually adore her, even when she has full-on conversations with bones. Mila is unusual, that's it.

"Yum," Raya exclaims, plopping down in the chair beside me. Her fork dives right for the tartar. A huge jiggly bite goes right into her mouth, sending a fresh wave of nausea bubbling in my gut. "So good." She licks the fork with the evilness only a sibling could muster.

She relishes the thought of getting her badge before me. Not that I can let that happen.

The shame of being lapped by my little sister has me reaching for the fork.

Almost.

I'm saved by the appearance of Director Cooper. She points a finger at me before hooking her thumb over her shoulder.

"You're coming with me." She has all the seriousness of a woman on a mission.

I mumble goodbyes to my family members, wondering how worse things are about to get.

Alyce doesn't speak a word to me until we are in her office with the door closed behind us. She leans against her desk and crosses her arms. She's formidable. She drips authority and power as she stands there, assessing me.

"I'm furious with you."

"Yes, ma'am."

"I don't like being lied to, and your omission was basically a lie."

"I'm sorry, ma'am."

"Oh, you will be."

My heart sinks. Maybe since our conversation yesterday, she's changed her mind, and now she wants to kick me out of the Academy for real.

"Sit." She nudges her chin toward one of the chairs. I sink into it, grateful to give my trembling legs a break. "I have your first assignment."

I straighten my back and plaster on an unaffected mask, but inside I'm doing a series of cartwheels. "Thank you, Director Cooper. I won't let you down."

"Did I say first assignment?" She clicks her tongue. "My bad. What I meant was, I'm sending you out on a test. Basically a babysitting mission. There shouldn't be any bloodshed."

Her large eyes watch me, studying my face for a reaction. I brought this on myself, I know that, but it doesn't make it any less painful. I don't know how to respond, so I merely nod.

"We'll talk about your status as an agent as soon as you return."

"So I'm not an agent?"

Her glowering look is all of the answer I need.

"Right."

"Take comfort in the fact that because of you, from now on, we are checking cadets for reactions to blood."

I wring my fingers together. *Yikes.* I can't defend my actions. Not in the least. Director Cooper is right to be worried. What would've happened to me if I passed out during a call? I could've gotten myself or my partner seriously hurt if I passed out at the wrong moment.

"You'll be spending the next little while with an important witness. He isn't necessarily in *that* much danger, but he needs to be kept alive at all costs. Do you understand me?"

"Yes, Director Cooper."

"Good. While you're babysitting this whistleblower, maybe you can train yourself to be around blood. Just make sure it's not Dr. Norbert Palomer's blood. We definitely need him alive."

With a wave of her hand, she dismisses me without giving me further details.

Not that any of it matters. Director Cooper is giving me a chance to redeem myself, and I won't squander it. Whatever she asked of me, I will gladly do it if it leads to a badge at the end of the assignment.

I'm back in business!

4

NORBERT

My log cabin, a small little structure I built with my own two hands, stands in the middle of a forest right by a spring. There's a natural break in the trees where I planted loads of fruits, vegetables, flowers, and basically anything I need to survive.

It's my haven.

No one knows where this place is. It doesn't have an address in the conventional sense, and it's off-grid.

I've got electricity, but it's all powered by sustainable energy. Sun, elbow grease, that kind of stuff. The internet is spotty, only accessible at a specific time of night when the earth's orbit passes over a specific satellite. I was lucky to be willed down this spot, one of the perks of being the son of two environmentalists with an eye on land and resource preservation.

Not that my parents would be proud of me if they were alive.

I'm in a right pickle.

Everything they taught me went out of the window. And for what? All because my ego got the best of me.

That and my dick.

Point out a man who doesn't get overly excited when his boss taps him for a special and *super*-secret project, and I will show you a damn liar. But, of course, seven months ago, I didn't know *why* the research was special and secret.

Now I know.

Replace special with *maniacal* and secret with *illegal*.

Quick tip: if something sounds too good to be true, it most definitely is.

Lisbeth Bannon made it all sound so damn simple. All I had to do was tweak my research from beauty products to medicine.

Well, medicine adjacent.

Just unlock the secret of immortality.

Lisbeth Bannon and her rich cronies want to live forever.

If we hadn't been sleeping together, Lisbeth *never* would have learned about my parents—how they died from some mysterious illness that had no name and definitely no cure. She dangled some pretty powerful and motivating stuff over my old wound.

You could save other people from diseases, Norbert. All kinds of illnesses could be cured and completely eradicated from existence because of you.

I fell for her bullshit hook, line, and sinker.

That's what I get for interacting with *people* again.

I get roped into a scheme so nefarious I'm now a prisoner in my own home. I have to let an agent live with me.

I hope whoever this dude is, he keeps to himself. Hell, maybe he'll be okay with throwing up a tent and hunkering down in the great outdoors. Protective custody doesn't have to mean that I've got to share my territory. It's not like my cabin has space for another soul, anyway.

There's one bedroom. One bed. One tiny bathroom. Everything is powered by my personal army of solar panels.

I've got acres of beautiful forest to explore. Thankfully, it's also my security system. My little house and farm are so deep in the woods that no one can find me unless they have my direct GPS coordinates.

The only person who has them now is Agent Val Downer.

I'm out on a ledge with this, and if whistleblowing kills me, it'll be because I trusted the wrong person.

Again.

With a series of grumbles, I slide on my boots and plaid shirt. My crops and gardens need some tender loving care. It's not their fault I've gone and fucked up my life.

I follow the path from my front porch to the back of the house. The small barn—a red shed, really—holds all of the equipment, but I bypass it, heading straight for my gardens. I'm pleased to see that everything is growing just fine. There are slugs wreaking havoc on my lettuce, but that's to be expected. I mostly plant it for them, anyway.

As a vegetarian, I've got to eat something more substantial than salads. That's why I've got an actual pumpkin patch. It's more of a *gourd* patch. All manners of squashes grow there. They're a great source of protein, and they're easy enough to grow.

Their outer protective shells are precisely why I picked *them* for my experiments. As much as I love all plants, I don't trust those that grow bare and vulnerable.

Strawberries are delicious, and they're rampant. Plant one bush of them, and you're sure to be overrun with the weed.

Biologically, it makes sense. It's such a fragile fruit; it has to be a persistent grower lest it is completely destroyed.

Plants with protective layers just make more sense to me. They're just as easy to grow, but I don't have to worry about them.

Sort of like how I don't have to worry about myself out here in the wilderness.

I might be a pumpkin, my skin is thick.

That's a whole other problem I need to fix.

If I have to be a pumpkin, I'd rather be sentient instead of morphing into a literal defenseless *thing*.

As I inspect my crops, I let my mind wander. This is where I do some of my best thinking. A nice long walk through my field usually sparks some kind of idea. I'm in serious need of some inspiration.

"Oh, you are parched, my darlings," I coo to a row of corn. I remove my finger from the dry soil and tut. If it doesn't rain soon, I'll have to use my rain barrels to water my harvest if I want to eat in the next few months.

For another little while, I roam and inspect, still clinging to the hope that something will pop into my mind.

There's nothing.

I'm way too distracted by my meeting with Val Downer. Giving her all of the information and files I have on Vitality Holdings was the right thing to do, but it also put me in hot water.

Not the pleasant kind found in the warm spring.

Nope.

The kind that will flay my hide raw.

My satellite phone is tucked in my back pocket, not a usual thing, but I'm eager to hear back from Agent Downer. She dropped *protective custody* like it was nothing.

It's not.

It's terrifying.

I've got to be careful now when I'm nervous. It's dangerous for my health—and my secret.

As if the koala shifter senses my thoughts, the phone goes off.

"There's an agent on the way," Agent Downer says by way of greeting. "Should be there sometime today. FUC will be sending some supplies later, too. I'll check in on you every now and again, but please keep a low profile."

I snort because Agent Downer has never seen my home, and it shows. There is no one around for miles and miles. "I'll make sure to hide from the family of squirrels that's taken residence in my shed."

"This isn't a joke, Norbert. If Bannon finds you…"

"I know." *Fuck, do I.* A shudder works its way up my spine.

You know what feels great? Being a fully grown man who has to hide because his ex is a psycho killer with *actual* plans for world domination.

I sure know how to pick 'em.

After disconnecting the call, I head back to my cabin and plop onto my sofa and look down at my crotch. "You're not to get us into trouble again, do you hear me? It's Mistress Palm for the rest of our lives now. Hope that makes you happy."

I throw my head back and focus on the wood grain of the overhead wood beams. The latticework makes me ache.

Everything in this world is connected by life's tendrils. Every single *thing* is linked to everything else.

I have to sever myself even more from that. As lonely and as alone as I've been for most of my life, I've learned my lessons now.

Those ties and bonds only lead to trouble and bullshit heartache.

It's not like I loved Lisbeth. That's not why my chest

hurts. What makes my inside want to jump ship is the betrayal. It boils in the marrow of my bones.

There is an easy solution.

I am *never* going to trust another human. Ever.

Fuck loneliness.

I'll just expand my garden. Plants don't let you down.

5

VERA

When Director Cooper gave me coordinates—not an address—I got a little excited. My heart fluttered with hope because she trusted me with a mission, but now that I'm looking at a dirt path suffocated by overgrown shrubs and arching tree branches, I'm not entirely sure she isn't playing a prank on me or something.

That's not exactly her style, but I'm not too keen on turning down a road that isn't actually a road that leads to potentially nowhere.

The GPS is *adamant* that I turn right.

I am *adamant* that I am about to die by driving off the ledge of a steep cliff.

What would Chase Brownsmith do?

He'd go.

Of course he would because he is a professional and a trained FUC agent who believes in his capabilities. I might not be an agent *yet*, and I definitely have no faith in my abilities, but I can fake it.

No one is around to see that my hands tremble on the steering wheel. I can just turn the wheel a few degrees to the right. I can do that. I can turn the armored car toward the direction of the GPS and go babysit a witness.

Flaming guano.

I don't know why I'm so nervous as the SUV hops and stumbles on the rough road. Every time I'm jarred, my gut reminds me that it's there, full of acid and an impressive projectile capacity.

The moon, nothing but a fingernail clipping in the dark, cloudy sky, is no help at all. The farther I drive, the more I hunch over the wheel as the shadows draw me in. I'm not scared of the nighttime—I'm nocturnal.

I *am* terrified of buffing this up. *That* equals never getting my badge. Failure is simply not an option for me.

Panic settles like a best friend in my sternum. The aching flutters pull up a seat in my brain, kick back, and relax like they own the place.

I am a bat. Hear me echolocate.

Say it three times fast and hope you believe the lie.

Finally, after three-hundred-and-two hours, I spot it.

A small log cabin pops out from the line of trees. There are no lights on inside, which isn't exactly surprising, given the late hour. Dr. Norbert Palomer is probably asleep at nearly eleven p.m.

I didn't get many details about him, but I'm expecting an older man. Maybe a hippie in his seventies, a throwback to another generation. I only hope that my arrival doesn't give the man a heart attack. Scaring my charge to death doesn't exactly scream *I'm a wonderful agent.*

With hands doing their best impressions of a paint shaker, I park the vehicle and grab my duffel bag, swinging it over my shoulder. A quick glance at the obscure house and its surroundings reveals very little about Dr. Palomer.

Director Cooper didn't exactly tell me *why* he is to be in

our protection. All I know is that I must protect the fragile human.

I roll my shoulders back and rap my knuckles on the wooden door three times. The taps reverberate in the night, but there is no sign of life within. Then, with more gusto than necessary, I knock again.

Nothing.

A shaky breath stutters out of me. "Dr. Palomer, I've been sent by the Cryptozoian Council and FUC. I'm Agent Slaski." Okay, so that's a lie, but he doesn't need to know that.

Still nothing.

What if the old man is dead? What if someone already got to him?

I drop my duffel on the porch swing and crack my knuckles before grabbing the door handle. A wiggle and a jiggle tell me it's unlocked.

Not a good sign.

I push my way in, letting my eyes do the work. There don't appear to be any light switches, which isn't a surprise. I didn't expect this place to have electricity. Not that I *need* a light source.

My night vision is pretty great as a nocturnal creature, but that's not my real secret weapon. I click my tongue against my teeth and wait silently as the echo builds an image in my mind.

That's all it takes for me to know the layout of the cabin. There's a small living room to my right. One plaid couch, one massive coffee table with books and papers piled precariously high. To the left are a bedroom and bathroom. I'm shocked that both are empty.

Another click of my teeth as I walk on toward the kitchen uncovers a door that leads down.

Huh.

I didn't expect a basement in a secluded log cabin.

"Dr. Palomer?" I call down the stairs as I step into the thick obscurity. "I'm here to protect you." A snort bubbles out of me. What a weird thing to say. "I've been sent by your contact, Val Downer."

The stairs end in a narrow hallway with a single direction: a steel door. The hairs on the back of my neck stand, making me shiver.

A door in a subterranean corridor doesn't exactly announce *this is safe*.

It actually reminds me of serial killers and cannibals.

"Hello?" I ask for the thousandth time, pushing my way through the heavy door.

There is no answer.

I run my hands along the wall, my fingers hitting against a nob. I turn it a quarter turn, and somewhere off in the distance, the whir of a generator kicks into life.

Overhead, a few bulbs blink into life, slowly unveiling a sizable room that's half lab, half greenhouse. The walls, gray concrete, match the stainless-steel countertops. The back of the space is overrun with huge plants, long and vibrant green shrubs, which I could never name.

"What is this guy *into*?" I mumble, continuing my exploration.

The lab is deserted save for an enormous pumpkin in the middle of the room. I kneel down and poke at it, the bright orange hue way too vivacious to be natural.

The large gourd squeaks a human and living sound.

I stumble back, my hand going to my chest in shock.

What the guano?

The squash shimmies and vibrates as it lets loose another squeal.

Demonic pumpkin!

This is how I die. Killed by a possessed gourd.

Taking a step back, I nearly fall flat on my ass. I steady myself, gripping the stainless-steel counter.

"I'm Agent Vera Slaski from FUC. I'm looking for Dr. Norbert Palomer."

I've lost my mind. I am talking to a pumpkin. If Chase Brownsmith could see me now…

Any good agent would have been scanning the lab for signs of intrusion or for the good doctor, but I'm riveted—and okay, a lot terrified.

The giant veg isn't behaving like any other plant I've ever seen.

Vegetation doesn't *have* behavior.

Yet there the pumpkin goes, vibrating like it's filled with cell phones and bees and vibrators.

"Hell—" My greeting dies when the explosion happens.

A loud *splat* sends wet and cold pumpkin guts scattering everywhere in the lab. My horrified gasp strangles itself when I finally manage to wipe pumpkin goo from my eyes.

Standing in the orange carcass is a very tall, very *naked* man.

6

VERA

The naked Pumpkin Man stands there, in all his buff glory, blinking at me in shock.

"Dude!" I turn, slapping my hands over my eyes.

It's too late, though. I've seen *it*.

Oh, sweet heavenly gourd.

"Who are you, and how did you get in here?" His baritone voice sparks tiny shivers up my spine.

"I'm Agent Vera Slaski." My voice trembles because there is a nude man behind me. A very *au naturel* and very attractive man.

Did he just climb out of a pumpkin?

Do. Not. Panic. If you can turn into a two-ounce bat, there's going to be a logical, scientific explanation for this.

"I've been sent by FUC," I continue, my tone as wobbly as my legs. "I came in through the front door, which wasn't locked. I was concerned for Dr. Palomer. Would you happen to know if he's around?"

"I'm doct—" He sighs. "I'm Norbert."

Hell to the no.

There's not a chance in this wild world that the person I

was sent to protect is Pumpkin Man. "Think you could put some clothes on?"

He mumbles something under his breath, but I don't quite catch it.

"I'm decent."

He most certainly is *not* decent.

Dr. Norbert Palomer has wrapped a small towel—the *smallest towel known to man*—around his trim waist. Above it is a deep V, planes and valleys of abdominal muscles that have no place on a Norbert. Soft black hair pulls my focus back down to his towel-covered area.

Nope. Eyes up, Agent.

Only, that isn't helpful.

His pecs are as toned and defined as his abs, and his shoulders are so wide and strong I have the urge to *bite* into the corded muscle.

Me. Broken bat that I am, I want to nibble on him like my favorite snack.

Flaming guano bomb, but this isn't good.

He runs a hand through thick, lush black curls, brushing the hair away from his deep and fiery hazel eyes. He grabs a pair of glasses from the counter and slides them up his patrician nose, blinking frantically at me.

Look, I am not the kind of woman who swoons or loses her mind over a dude. I reserve that for blood.

I haven't had a boyfriend in nearly three years, nor have I felt any compulsion to tie myself to the opposite sex.

But.

I've never exactly seen a man like Dr. Norbert Palomer— especially not *nude.*

It is exceedingly hot down here. It *has* to be a hothouse or something. I wish I could fan my face for a bit of relief.

"What are you doing here?" he asks, opening a cupboard.

"FUC sent me."

He turns toward me, and his bespeckled gaze takes me all in. I gulp because—*sweet, suffering mammal*—he is one intense man.

"They sent *you*?" he snorts and, with a twirling finger, demands that I turn. "Do they even understand the danger I'm in?" he says to my back.

"Meaning what, exactly?" My temper flares, twinging my retort with sass. "I assure you, Doctor. I am more than capable of protecting you from whatever threat you face. Even exploding pumpkins."

"Vera, you said?"

"Yes." *Ouf.* He draws out the *a*, turning it into an *ah* that evokes dirty, naughty, sweaty flutters in my nether region.

"Do you know why I need protective custody?"

"Yes."

He chuckles. "I really doubt they told you everything."

"Well." This guy. Arrogant, much? "I have to keep you alive long enough so that you can testify in a trial. I don't know why exploding pumpkins are part of this, but there you have it."

"I'm not an exploding pumpkin. You can face me, by the way."

I turn, ready to reply, but my mind is as lost as a bat in a tanning bed.

Norbert has covered his dangler and other enticing bits with a pair of black jeans so faded they might as well be gray, a white tee, and a red plaid shirt, unbuttoned with the sleeves rolled up to his elbows.

Note to self: forearms can be erotically charged.

"Do you often garden in your underground lab in the

dark while nude?" The words blurt out of me, and I go twenty shades of red.

"I wasn't gardening." He runs a hand back through his hair, but the stubborn curl that loops over his forehead takes position again. He huffs out a breath to remove it, but it's no use. "You're sworn to secrecy while you're here, right?"

"Basically, but if you murder someone, I'll have to arrest you."

Norbert—I really need to find him a better name— purses full lips at me. How a pair of lips can be so damn captivating framed by a short black beard, I've got no clue. The good doctor has this whole '90s grunge vibe going. It would have made teenage Vera loopy for the bad boy.

Only he's not a bad boy.

He's a fully grown man under my charge. Maybe I should stop ogling.

"I wasn't gardening. The lights are on a timer. They go out when there's no movement for ten minutes."

Something prickles at the base of my neck. "*Steaming blood bag*," I gasp. "You were the pumpkin?" I shake my head, clearing the webs of insanity weaving my thoughts together. "*You* were *in* the *pumpkin*?"

He bristles and crosses those sexy, muscular, veiny arms. "I wasn't in the pumpkin. I *am* the pumpkin."

I blink at him. "I'm sorry. You shift into *vegetation*?" I shake my head once again. "No. That's impossible. There's no way."

"I don't have the time or desire to explain, but yes. I shift into a pumpkin when under threat."

"You turn into a pumpkin when you're scared?" What in the damn hell has Director Cooper gotten me into?

"No." His hazel eyes narrow into angry slits. "Not when I'm *scared*. When I'm *threatened*."

"Isn't that the same thing?"

"Absolutely not." He puffs out his chest. "Scared if when I feel *fear*. Threatened is different. More like a threat is *right* in front of me, or I'm in danger."

"Sounds like the same thing to me."

"Well, it's not."

"So if I were to threaten you right now, you'd turn into a jack-o'-lantern?" I grab a scalpel from the counter and point it at him. "Get on with it, Cinderella."

"Don't," he growls. "It's no laughing matter."

I want to make a joke about pumpkin spice. Something like, *Rub your spice all over me, Jack*, but I decide against it.

Suddenly, being a non-agent, a broken bat who can't ingest blood, all of that vanishes. I'm not the only fucked-up person in the world.

It's comforting.

It's also a little bit attractive.

There is some cosmic thing, some impossible-to-decipher pull, binding us together.

"Explain to me how a grown man can morph into a gourd."

"No. I can't, and I won't. It can't be common knowledge, so forget that you even saw that."

I take in the pumpkin guts still scattered across the lab. "Unlikely to happen. I need to know how to deal with this in case we come under attack."

"Agent Vera, my predicament is none of your concern." He continues, spewing all kinds of scientific terms that go way above my head. Maybe if Mila was here, she'd understand.

I lift a hand. "Okay, Jack. Enough with the blabbering. If you don't tell me what the hell happened here, I'll grind you up for my next latte." *You'll be delicious; I just* know *it*.

I think my comment is hilarious. He does *not*.

Jack pushes his glasses up his long, slender nose, the brightness of his gaze burning through the thick lens. "I'd prefer if you called me by my name."

"Which is?" I already forgot it. I dub him Jack, and he will forever be known as nothing else in my mind.

Jack, the Nude King in the Pumpkin Patch.

"Norbert," he reminds me uselessly.

"Right, well, don't get your plaid in a twist. Explain the pumpkin thing."

"It's late. We should get to bed."

"I'm nocturnal," I snicker. "It's basically early morning for me. I've got all night to chat." I smile at him sweetly.

His scowl isn't sexy *at all*. Not even when that stubborn forehead tendril quivers from his annoyance.

"Come on, Jack," I tease, hopping onto the counter. "Tell me how you became the Pumpkin King."

7

NORBERT

Agent Vera Slaski hops onto the stainless-steel counter, crosses one leg over the other, and props up her head by cupping her cheek. Her perfect Cupid's bow, painted pink and glossy, turns up into a smile.

Do not be pulled in.

Her eyes are a shade of hazel that flirts with amber and emerald. Every time she blinks her long inky lashes, I get a new color show that makes me want to lean in and study her.

She's an agent. A shifter.

I. Do. Not. Trust. People.

Her brown hair is short, barely brushing against her shoulders, but it's thick and a shade so rich it reminds me of melted chocolate. I want to bury my face in it and take a whiff. I bet it smells better than any damn thing in this world.

Stand the fuck down, Norbert, you absolute perv.

After everything that's happened with Lisbeth Bannon and Vitality Holdings, I am definitely *not* ready to trust another human.

Or another shifter, as this case may be.

I'm not about to spill all of my secrets to an agent that will have to report everything I say to her superiors.

There's every chance that I'll be charged and jailed if FUC and the Cryptozoian Council ever figure out just how involved I was with all of the testing and research.

As noble as I was raised to be, I don't have a burning need to be locked behind bars because of an experiment gone wrong.

It's not like I hurt anyone. Only myself—and a few pumpkins.

"You really won't tell me how you came to be a pumpkin?"

"No."

"But what if it's information I need to protect you?"

"It won't be," I assure her.

"Well, at the very least, tell me what I need to do if you do turn into a great big veg again."

"Pumpkins are fruit, actually," I mutter. "It's a seed-bearing fruit. Not a vegetable. To the point, it's a gourd, which in tu—" I stop blathering when I spot the grin on Vera's face.

By rakes and hoes, she's lovely.

That's a dangerous thought.

I can't stand there, melting and going all gooey for the FUC agent here to defend me should Vitality Holdings send a hit man or six. Not when I have to keep so many things secret.

But she already knows one of them. What's another?

Nope. Not happening.

Vera Slaski, with the pretty lips, lush hair, and shining eyes, is definitely the last person I will—can—trust.

"I have quite the imagination, you know," she says. "I'll

just make up something." She taps her chin, scrunching up her button nose in a cute way that has my male equipment perking up. "When a mommy pumpkin and a daddy pumpkin grow in the same patch—"

"I beg of you, stop." I rip my glasses off to pinch the bridge of my nose.

"Once upon a time, there was a botanist. He grew all kinds of gourds. One day, he noticed that—"

"It was an accident," I grumble, and Vera finally lapses into a beat of silence.

"You accidentally turned yourself into a gourd?"

"Well, yes and no. I was doing some minor experiments, and things got out of hand."

"So you don't have a full family growing in that garden then? You're a real boy, Pinocchio?"

"I'm a real man," I amend because let's be real. Vera saw me in the nude. If she thinks my hardware isn't all man, maybe she didn't get a good enough look.

Maybe I need to remedy that.

Fascinated, I watch as an adorable blush creeps up Vera's cheeks. She tucks her brown hair behind her ears, her hand landing at the base of her throat.

"I can't give you any more details than that." My voice is gravel and sand. I can't stop staring at the pink hue of her lovely face.

"And so you explode every time you shift back into a human?"

I tense. "Not quite."

"I get the sense that you don't trust me. I understand, I do. You don't know me, and obviously, if you need protective custody, it means that you might have some paranoia."

"I'm not paranoid."

"Right. Well, I was a lawyer before I became an agent.

How about we operate under the pretense that we have attorney-client privileges? Whatever you share stays between the two of us."

"Unless I murder someone," I shoot back, throwing her earlier words back at her.

"Exactly. Though, if there is a threat, please let me deal with that. I've got a license to kill." She winks, and I swear, all the oxygen whooshes out of me.

No. Nope, Norbert. Avert your eyes. This siren is not for you.

"What kind of shifter are *you*?" I ask in hopes of turning the attention away from myself.

"Vampire bat," she answers with a shrug. "Mini but mighty, I assure you."

"A vampire bat?" I repeat.

"Yep."

"So you're about this big when you shift?" I cup my hands where a baby bird could easily nestle.

Vera nods. "Like I said, mini but mighty."

"And what if my enemies send a rhino or a bear? You'll duke it out with a huge, hulking predator?"

She leaps off the counter and stalks toward me. Vera isn't short, but I'm tall. Her head reaches just above my chin, but that doesn't stop her from trying to be intimidating. She jabs a finger into the center of my chest before pointing it at me.

"Listen here, Jack. *I'm* a predator. I have to drink blood every day to survive. I've got the sharpest incisors in the mammal world. My saliva has some anticoagulant particles. If I wanted to, I could bleed a one-ton bear dry in a matter of minutes."

For the first time in my life, anger and attraction get confused. Vera pokes my chest again. This time she keeps her finger pressed into me. The touch, reprimanding as it is, has no right being so damn sexy.

It is.

My dick notices all kinds of things about the batty lady.

There are gold and amber flecks in her eyes, and her brown hair shimmers like strands of cooper. Her lips are full and pink with the sweet scent of cotton candy. If I crushed Vera into my arms, all our good parts would line up and touch in a perfect greeting.

"Anything else you wanna say, *pumpkin*?"

"I'm going to bed," I announce.

Vera's gaze flashes, and her breath hitches. Or maybe that's my imagination. There's a tiny possibility that I'm attracted to the FUC agent.

That means I need to be a dick, set up some solid boundaries, and make sure Vera keeps her distance.

Should be easy enough for me to manage, given that I very rarely interact with other humans. They don't call me the Reclusive Botanist for nothing.

"We can have this whole night and day thing down. You do your guard duty thing while I sleep, and then I'll take the daytime hours. There's no need for us to interact at all."

I don't miss the hurt and disappointment that plays across Vera's features.

Okay, so maybe I'm not that comfortable being an ass with Vera Slaski, but that is exactly *why* I have to do it.

The last time I was pulled in by attraction, things didn't end so well for me. Or for the environment. Or for the entire human race.

"I'm gonna clean this up and hit the hay."

Vera makes her way out of the lab without looking back. If the basement wasn't soundproof, I would most likely hear her pacing the floor above me as I wipe down the floor, counter, and cupboards of pumpkin. Hell, some even found its way up to the ceiling. I probably spend too much time cleaning up my shifter mess, but better that than another charged exchange with my keeper.

It's nearly midnight by the time I climb up the stairs. Vera is nowhere to be seen, and I assume she's gone to take a lap around the property.

Good.

It's better that way.

I complete my nighttime ablutions playing a new game: thought ping pong.

Every two seconds, an image of Vera pops into my brain, forcing me to lop at it. But it bounces back, gathering speed and clarity while I brush my teeth and change into a pair of pajama bottoms. I close the bedroom door behind me before Vera can return from whatever agent business she's taking care of.

Even if she *is* an agent, I don't feel right making her sleep on the couch. It's not exactly the most comfortable surface. Maybe we can share the bed.

At the thought, my dick stirs and starts to thicken, but I knock the thought far away.

Ping.

It whips round right back at me, whipping my brain as if I were playing against a pro.

Not share-share, I explain to myself like a true squash-brained dude. *We won't be in bed at the same time.*

Since I've already established that Vera can keep her nocturnal hours, we can both use the bed. At different times. Not together.

Not even if she finds a way into my dreams. I'll ping pong that to the depths of hell before I dream of Vera Slaski.

8

VERA

As it turns out, babysitting a grown man is boring.

Even if said grown man is a complete *dish.*

Even if the complete dish turns into an enormous pumpkin.

Of all the damn things to shift into, a large orange gourd is the last thing anyone should want to morph into. Jack indicated that it happened by accident, but I'm not clear how that can even happen.

Granted, I'm no science buff, but it seems to me that I've walked into Frankenstein's lab. Only instead of creating a dude out of decomposing bodies, Jack has turned himself into a Halloween cartoon character.

I want to ask more questions, but he has managed to dodge me like an expert in the last twenty-four hours. As soon as I woke up, he went to bed.

He wouldn't use my nocturnal hours to avoid me.

I made sure to get to bed early when the sun was still up, so I would have a few hours with my charge.

No such luck.

I shifted on the super uncomfortable couch, and Jack

rushed to the bathroom. The shower kicked on, and before I even got a chance to imagine what it would look like to see Jack under the spray of hot water, he hurried by in nothing but plaid pajamas, slunk down on his hips.

He did that on purpose.

Or that's what I'm going with.

He *has* to know that the material stretches over his bubble butt.

He's *got* to know that the V disappearing into the waistband is *made* to scramble lady bits and brains.

Jack won't be able to hide from me for much longer. My severe sun allergy makes it difficult for me to change up my hours, but dusk isn't *too* painful. The man can't go to bed at seven and expect me to believe that he's in there catching Z's already.

Since our tense conversation in the basement lab, he hasn't said much to me.

"If you keep your nocturnal hours, you can have the bedroom while I'm up and about."

That was it

It was also clear as day the man *wanted* to avoid me.

It couldn't be easy, sharing his small cabin with a stranger, but we didn't have to keep on walking on eggshells around each other. Who knew how long it would take for FUC to complete their investigation into whatever Jack was mixed up in? Who knew how long it would be for his testimony to be needed?

I could be here for weeks. Months.

The man had to get over himself and get used to it.

To me.

The sun is still pretty high in the sky when I force myself awake. My head is woozy from lack of blood. I haven't had a sip of the stuff in days. I can only stomach it in my bat shape, and even then, it's hard to hunt. Harder to stomach the thick, life-giving liquid. Harder still to take back my human form without needing an hour-long shower, a gallon of antacids, and a liter of mouthwash.

There's nothing for it, though. I'll have to hunt some poor creature down tonight to get at least a teaspoon of blood.

The last thing I need is to be off my game because of my aversion to blood. That would hardly endear me to Director Cooper. Especially if we come under attack.

Psyching myself out for the gross meal, I get dressed, slipping on a pair of fuchsia leggings and a pale pink tee. Tucking my elongated bob into a half-pony is a challenge, but I don't waste precious time coiffing myself.

I am no longer a lawyer who needs to dress for success.

I am an agent. The rules are very different but *so* liberating.

I *almost* understand Raya's unaffected attitude. *Almost.*

"Good evening," I keep my tone chipper and friendly when Jack enters the cabin a few minutes later.

His graying black jeans are dusted with dirt, as are his white tee and green plaid shirt. His glasses, perched on the tip of his nose, are just as filthy. A streak of mud along his cheek matches a few others down his sinewy arms. I force air into my lungs, demanding that my brain settle.

Don't get your wings in a twist, V. He's only a dude. An everyday kind of dude with super sexy black curls and an ass that I could use as a chew toy.

Whoa.

The last thought is startling, making me squeak.

Weird. So weird. I definitely need to ingest some blood before I become a danger to Dr. Norbert *Jack* Palomer.

"You're up," he grumbles, walking straight for the

kitchen. He turns the tap on and scrubs his hands and forearms in the huge white sink. The soapy water glides over his
muscular arms as he turns back to give me a once-over.

I lean against the wall and watch him wash his skin raw.
"I'm up. I think it's ridiculous that we're avoiding each other
like the plague. This is a very small cabin, and who knows
how long I'll be here?"

Why did I frame that like a question?

I take a deep breath and try again. "We should try to be
civil."

"Civil." He repeats the world like it's a completely foreign
concept to him.

"Yup. You know, talk, maybe share a few meals. Maybe
even get to know each other."

"No, thank you."

My jaw drops. "What's *with* you? I get that you have this
whole quiet, broody farmer thing down, but I'm gonna go
insane if I don't have some kind of human connection in the
next few weeks."

Jack grabs a towel and dries his hands before balling it
up and throwing it onto the small kitchen table. "I'm not
used to having someone underfoot."

"No. Ya don't say."

He purses his lips. "I'm also not accustomed to long-
winded conversations."

"Or conversations at all," I volley back.

His eyebrow hooks this time, and there's the suggestion
of a smile on his lips.

"I get that you're a secretive dude. You're gonna testify
against a big evil corporation. I understand that. Only, I
don't, because my superiors didn't exactly give me a lot of
details and you haven't been forthcoming."

"You already know enough to seriously screw me over."

I frown, confused. "I won't tell anyone you're a pumpkin, Cinderella." I draw a cross over my heart before pretending to zip my lips. "I'm guessing you're sketchy about it because if FUC or the Cryptozoian Council found out, you'd face some serious repercussions."

He nods, his entire body tensing.

"If we both want to get out of this with our reputations intact, we need to work together. I call for a truce." I hold out my hand, but Jack looks at it like it's a pesticide bottle. I move my fingers expectantly, but he continues to stare.

"You'll stop calling me Cinderella?"

I scrunch up my nose. "If I must."

"And you'll drop the Jack thing?"

"I can try," I lie.

Am I going to tell this man I can't call him Norbert because I have a hard time imagining myself moaning out *Norbert*?

No.

Absolutely not.

I'm here on assignment. Not just any kind of assignment, but one that is meant to save my career before it can even start.

"If I tell you something *super* embarrassing about myself, will you explain to me how you turned yourself into a walkin'-talkin' Jack-o'-lantern?"

Jack inhales deeply and crosses his arms. "It'll have to be one hell of a good story."

"Why don't we sit down, have some breakfast or whatever meal you're at in your day, and chat. It's a normal thing to do, Jack. Sit and converse with whomever you're sharing lodgings."

"I'll park it, but only because you used *whomever* in a sentence and that's sexy."

My eyes pop out of my head. They're probably rolling on the ground somewhere along with my jaw. There is no air to be had for my poor, suffering lungs.

Jack called me sexy.

Sort of.

Judging by the crimson tint of his scruffy cheeks, he had *no* intention of making the comment. It popped out of his mouth before he could even stop it.

I grin at him, arching a brow in what I hope is a flirty, teasing way. I pass by him en route to the solar-panel-powered refrigerator, its loud hum the only sound in the cabin. It takes a decent amount of self-control not to brush up against him on purpose.

I grab milk, berries, and a box of cereal before settling at the table. I'm already scarfing down my meal when Jack decides to sit in front of me with his own bowl.

"Breakfast for dinner?" I ask.

He grunts his reply.

"So Norbert is an interesting name. Your parents pick it for any particular reason?"

"Not that I know of, no."

"Do *they* know how you turned yourself into a pumpkin?"

Jack shakes his head. "No. They're no longer with us."

"Oh. Shit. Sorry."

He shrugs, slurping a huge spoonful of cereal. "Before I get into any of that, you owe me *your* embarrassing tale. If I deem it worthy, I might share."

"It's worth it, all right." I push my bowl away and tap my fingers on the table. Sure, I don't *really* mind telling Jack that I can't ingest blood without needing smelling salts. Everyone knows now, so it's hardly this dark secret.

It's the embarrassment that stalls me.

Hey, hot farmer dude I barely know. Guess what? I'm broken, and I was only sent here to prove that I can be an agent without putting anyone's life in danger.

That wouldn't go over well, methinks.

With a deep sigh, I launch into the tale of the blood-hating vampire.

Jack listens intently, his eyes settling on me like I'm the most fascinating person in the world. That won't last long. As soon as he learns I need to ingest blood to survive, any possible attraction he has for me will evaporate.

It's probably for the best. Agents shouldn't want to strip their charges naked and ride them till the moon comes out.

Jack, King of the Pumpkin Patch, is way off-limits.

9

———

NORBERT

Vera is lovely.

She sits at my kitchen table—a place no woman has ever occupied before her—and she tells me her greatest shame. She is a vampire bat with an aversion to blood. Her flushed cheeks and misty eyes throat punch me. Her sadness is palpable. I reach over the table and squeeze her hand.

Why?

No idea.

My brain is probably turning into spaghetti squash.

"I'm sure you're not the only vampire bat that has reservations about blood." I grin at her with all of the comforting energy I can muster.

She purses her lips. That damn lip gloss of hers shimmies, catching the very low light in the kitchen. She smells like cotton candy. It shouldn't be an erotic aroma, but on her?

Well, it's a good thing there's a table between us and that we're not standing around the lab with me in my birthday suit. Vera would get a whole other view of me in *that* situation.

"You're sweet to say that, but there's no real proof."

"Proof," I scoff. "What's *your* pool of intel?"

"My whole family." She winces. "That includes Sveta Markov. She's my mom's sister."

I whistle low.

Shit, shit, double shit sandwich.

What are the chances that the Bloody Doctor's niece would end up being the agent charged with my safety? Is this some kind of cosmic joke? I'd love to know the punchline before it nuts me.

"Yikes. Seems to me that you don't like blood because your aunt kept more than her fair share of those genes."

"Huh. I never thought of it like that, but I do like that idea." Her smile is sweet and tentative.

"So why is this such a big deal, then?"

"It's embarrassing. I've passed out loads of times, including in front of my personal hero. Not to mention the pressure I feel to *get over it*. You know, I don't actually think I should get over it. I mean, I *have* to, but only because I feel like a broken bat."

"Hey, now. None of that."

Vera shakes her head, clearing her thoughts. Her movements scent the air with cotton candy, and my mouth waters. Would she taste like sugar if I kissed her? The thought has a vise grip on my balls.

"It's your turn, now. Come on, Jack. Tell me how this happened."

I lean back in my chair, crossing my arms. "I should make you sign an NDA or something."

"I was a lawyer. I assure you I can keep a secret."

"So long as no one gets killed," I finish for her.

She nods.

"I feel like we should pinky swear." *Or kiss on it.*

Damn it, Norbert. Keep your zucchini to yourself.

Vera leans over the table, pinky out and grinning wide. I crook my finger with hers and squeeze. Our gazes collide. They hook together like thunderclouds, electric and so *natural.* It steals the breath right out of my lungs.

"You gonna let me go, Jack?"

It'll be fucking hard, V.

I drop her finger to run my fingers through my hair. "This isn't a good story."

"You heard me say that my aunt is the Bloody Doctor, right?"

I wince. "Yeah..." *Shit. I wonder how she's going to react when she hears* that *part of my tale.* "I guess I have to start way back at the beginning."

"You mean when your parents decided to name you Norbert?"

"Something like that," I chuckle. Her eyes spark with humor. "So my parents, both brilliant botanists focused on resource protection and environmental changes, name me Norbert. I wasn't actually born here. I lived the first ten years of my life in the Amazonian rainforest. I didn't go to school, not conventionally, anyway. My parents taught me everything they knew. Everything I know."

"That must have been a lot of fun. Traipsing through all that wildlife."

I smile at her genuine enthusiasm. "It was a lot of fun, yeah. At least until my parents contracted a rare disease. To this day, no one knows what hit them. The best guess is that they played with genomes they weren't supposed to toy with."

She gasps. "Genomes?"

"Genes, yeah. They were botanists, but something of mad scientists, too."

"Hmm," she sighs, getting to her feet to clear away my dinner and her breakfast. "Now I see where you get it from."

"Right. I should have probably learned my lesson from their deaths, but I can't help myself. You give me a string of plant DNA and I wanna uncover all of its mysteries."

Vera's giggle is adorable. She settles back at the table, choosing the seat beside me instead of facing me. The heat of her leg caresses mine, and I should definitely move away. I don't. It's nice to be close to another person. To *her*.

"Go on, please." She draws her elbow onto the table and cups her cheeks, ready to listen some more.

"I followed in their path," I continue. "I became a botanist. I did my Ph.D. on the study of..." I stop myself short. "Well, that's boring. Basically, I was playing with plant genome."

"Sounds *fascinating*."

"It is. I was fine making a living here, researching and publishing some scientific papers every now and again. Last year, I was approached by a company. A major corporation. Top of the beauty industry, actually. They wanted to hire me to use my research to develop completely organic and plant-based products."

"Oh, that must have gotten your botanist zucchini *real* hard."

A deep laugh rolls out of me. "It sure did, though I wouldn't put it quite like that."

"I did it for you." She punctuates her thought with a wink that zings me right in my *actual* zucchini. Not the botanist one, the very real, very fleshy one.

I clear my throat and rub a hand over my mouth in hopes of covering my blush. "It all started fine. I was doing my work here by correspondence. Sending my research in. I had some good ideas, so I wasn't *too* surprised when the

CEO, Lisbeth Bannon, basically demanded that I make a visit to headquarters."

"Wait. Are you telling me you were working for Vitality?"

"Yeah." I'm not surprised she knows who they are. It's probably one of the biggest beauty companies in the world.

Now I know why, too. Those crooked bastards.

"What did she want?"

"She wanted to pull me from the project. The company was working on something else. Something secret but life-changing. They took my research and gave it to another employee. They didn't want me to muck about with plants anymore, but with DNA."

"A different kind of genome."

"Exactly."

"Human?" she guesses.

"*Shifter*," I correct.

Vera gasps and covers her mouth. "Jack, please tell me you did *not* mix shifter DNA with plant DNA and inject yourself with it."

"I mean, I don't have to *say* it if you don't want me to."

"But that's what you did."

I nod. "That's what I did."

"Of all the dumb things to do. You could've killed yourself."

"I reached the end of the work. I could do nothing more without testing theories. Science is all about taking chances and going for the big risk. I knew I couldn't die, exactly. But Vitality demanded results. They were insistent, and I could tell there was a rush on things. That if I didn't do what they needed me to do, they'd get someone else. It felt too signifi-cant to give up, though. And in the wrong hands, it could be bad. Very bad."

Vera narrows her eyes. "Why do I feel like you're keeping something big from me?"

Here was the rub: how much did I tell her?

Did I admit that Lisbeth and I got a little too friendly? Did I tell Vera that her aunt's research was involved? How far could I go before it was all too much for her? I already shared most of this with Agent Downer. My reservations are strictly because Vera is...

Truth be told, I don't understand why I give two tosses about what Vera thinks of me.

Lie. Such a lie. Good thing fibbing doesn't make an exploding pumpkin out of me.

"'Cause I am. Vitality was dumping toxic waste in a few spots. One not too far from here, actually. I was livid. I went right back to Lisbeth Bannon and told her about it. She promised they would stop. She insisted she had *no* idea it was even happening but that she would get to the bottom of it. A month went by, and it happened again. That's when I called the Cryptozoian Council. I knew they would be the only ones who could help me because Bannon and the rest of the Vitality bigwigs are shifters." *Sort of.*

"All this is about toxic waste? Not about you messing around with shifter DNA?"

This is it. The moment that decides how much I tell her.

There's so much hopeful expectation in her eyes. Not to mention that I feel like a damn fool for falling into such a basic trap.

"That's it," I lie.

It rolls off my tongue like it's nothing, but it's not.

Vera's right to call me Cinderella. Eventually, the clock *will* strike midnight, the pumpkin will blow, and it won't be pretty.

10
———

NORBERT

A truce.

That's the only thing that can ever be between Vera and me.

A temporary agreement between a FUC agent and a witness in protective custody is where the buck stops for us.

By rights, the second she told me she needs blood to survive—that she is the Bloody Doctor's niece—I should have asked her to leave. I should've pretended to be grossed out and scared that I'd wake up in the middle of the night with Vera sucking on my neck.

But of course, the thought of her climbing into my bed, straddling me, pinning me down into the bed elicits other kinds of reactions—specifically below the belt.

That's probably the only reason why I rush through my daily chores around the crops. Usually, I drag it out, taking my own sweet time.

Sometimes I even stay and chat with the plants. Not because I'm a psycho but because I like to explain why I sheer them every now and again.

I don't do any of that today.

Not only did I get a later start after changing my hours to overlap a bit with Vera's, but there's an excited energy thrumming inside of me as I imagine spending a few hours chatting with her. I've always been solitary, but Vera turned the lights on in my cabin. Not the real, solar-powered lights.

Metaphorical ones that illuminated the lonely shadows that have always been my companions.

She's been here just over forty-eight hours and she's already changed my life in small but irrevocable ways.

When all of this business with Vitality Holdings ends, Vera will have to leave. Something will be left behind, though. Knowledge that as much as I claim to enjoy my life as a reclusive subsistence farmer, having someone around is okay.

If that person is Vera? Even better.

I wipe my filthy hands down the front of my jeans, but they're a dirty mess. It's not like I can make myself presentable in the small barn by the pumpkin patch. I shouldn't even be *thinking* like this.

A truce.

That's all we have.

I keep her secret, and she'll keep the one I shared.

I kick off my boots by the door and shrug out of my plaid shirt. My white tee sticks to my dewy skin; I've nearly sweat through the thing. I must smell horrible, but maybe we need that buffer between us.

Vera stands in the kitchen, her curves wrapped in bright blue leggings and a neon pink tee. Her hair, shorter in the back and longer in the front, is all smooth and silky. My fingers itch to run along the strands, but I'm filthy.

Not to mention I *lied* to her last night. The omission is one massive weight around my neck. I push it out of my mind.

So what if I'm attracted to Vera? She's only here because it's her job. I don't *owe* her anything. Besides, I'm a grubby, reclusive subsistence farmer. If I were to be all, *Hey, so my sort-of ex also manipulated me into doing research into immortality*, Vera would bolt faster than a clock could strike twelve.

"Morning," I say to her from the sink.

She doesn't respond but continues scowling at the kitchen table. A small metallic cylinder sits in the very center, but why she's staring at it like it's about to sprout legs and walk away, I don't know.

"What the hell is *that*?"

"Blood." Her shoulders tremble at the mere thought of it.

"It's not a bomb, V."

Her sneer turns teasing as she looks in my direction. "Oh, but it sure feels like it. Director Cooper sent over some supplies while you were out working. She included *this* to prove a point."

"Blood is a point to make?" I ask, already knowing the answer.

"Most definitely. The canister thingy is ingenious, don't you know. It keeps the blood at precisely the right heat to mimic the average blood temperature of a mammal."

Gross. So gross.

I'm hardly going to tell Vera that her basic functional needs are a tad repulsive. She knows. It's also not her fault, and I'm the very last person to judge.

"Is there anything I can do to help you with this?"

She shakes her head. "Nope. Either I drink it or toss it and have to find some source of blood soon."

"What do you mean?"

Vera purposefully avoids my gaze. "Because I haven't ingested any in a while, and that's sort of dangerous for bats like me."

I thump my way over to the table and grab the receptacle. It's surprisingly warm to the touch. "What if we mix it in spaghetti sauce or something?"

Her mouth drops into a perfect O when she gasps. "And ruin spaghetti forever? You're out of your gourd. No way, Jack. I'll just have to hunt tonight." She clutches her stomach and goes green in the face at the mere thought of it.

It sparks an idea in the back of my mind. "You won't drink this?"

As pale as an unripened ash gourd, she mumbles, "I have to toss it."

"I'm gonna go work in the lab for a bit while you figure out how you'll track down prey large enough to survive without a teaspoon of blood. Let me know when you're back."

Vera nods and retreats to the bathroom while I make my way to the lab.

If I can find the answer to immortality in human blood, I'm sure I can find a way to make *something* that will fulfill Vera's needs without making her queasy.

"And?" I ask Vera a few hours later.

It's almost midnight, and she's brushing her teeth for the second time since I emerged from the lab. She shakes her head, holding out a finger before vanishing into the bathroom.

"I hate, hate, *hate* it. I will never get used to it."

"Your parents must've had a fine time getting you to take your blood."

She nods emphatically. "You've got no idea. It's was bad, too, 'cause my little sister Raya would pipe up. *I drank my blood.* It was her point of pride. She was the good daughter. The *better* daughter because she didn't fight them every day. She drove me nutso bananas all the time about it."

"Your aversion to blood doesn't mean you're a bad daughter."

Vera settles onto the couch, curling her legs under her. "I had to fly pretty far to find something decent." She completely ignores my comforting line. Maybe it wasn't enough, or maybe I'm clumsy with my words. "Poor moose," she goes on. "At least he didn't even feel it. How was the lab? Did you turn yourself into a pumpkin?" I want to kiss her smirk.

Wait. What? I do?

Oh, I definitely fucking do.

"Nope." I take a seat beside Vera. There's a good two feet between us, but I long to be closer. Her pink lips are *right* there. Not that I'll actually kiss her. Ever. "Doing a bit of research on another project. Unrelated to my situation."

"Can you reverse your gourd problem?"

"Unlikely. The formula rewrote my genetic code."

"So any time you're threatened, you're gonna go all orange and defenseless?"

I wince. "Unless I can figure out what to add to my DNA, yes."

"Add?" she gasps. "Is this a *joke*? You can't *add*. You've already turned yourself into vegetation. What's next?"

"You don't wanna know."

Her eyes go wide. "But I really do. I'm kinda terrified that I'll walk into the lab one day and find a pumpkin with legs and arms."

"If I get things my way, that's exactly what will happen."

"What a nightmare. A scarecrow with a pumpkin head."

"Huh. Now there's an idea. That could be how to make my gourd sentient. I wonder if there is something…"

Vera smacks my leg. "Do not even go there."

I grip her fingers. The playful touch is anything but innocent to the southern parts of me. "Jack Scarecrow could be my shifter alter ego."

She giggles. "Hey, now. That's not so bad. It would also go with your whole vibe." She motions toward my body—or maybe my clothes.

Please let it be my body.

"Yeah," she goes on. "The grungy bad boy farmer thing you've got going on."

"Bad boy, huh?" I can't help it. I lean into her. Two feet becomes one. "You ever into the bad boys?" One foot becomes an inch.

She grins, sly and cute and way too close. Her hand draws up my thigh. "Nope. I like the studious types. You know, always in the library with glasses on the tip of their nose." She punctuates her breathy line by poking my nose.

My anatomy is suddenly very interested in the tip of my nose. It's not an erogenous zone, but damn it all to hell if her fingertip on me doesn't feel like the most erotic sensation.

I swallow hard as my dick stirs happily.

Mistress Palm? More like Mistress Bat.

I try to shrug the thought away, but it's too late. Vera is *right* there, simmering my blood with her hazel eyes and tempting lips. I want to say something clever, flirt back.

I've got nothing.

It's probably for the best. So what if she's gorgeous and sweet? She's an agent sent to keep watch over me. I can't get myself into any more trouble. Vera is nothing like Lisbeth, but that doesn't mean I should lean into the trust.

"Jack?" Vera's voice is raspy, evoking all kinds of naughty things. "Can I have my hand back?"

Stunned, I look down to see that I'm holding onto her hand, our fingers woven together. I let go and jump to my feet. "Gotta go check on the gourds."

I slam the front door behind me in hopes of shaking loose the desire pulsing inside me. I lumber to the pumpkin patch with the stars blinking above me in the dark blue sky.

Have I really not learned my lesson?

Note to self: don't sit close to Vera.

Don't touch her. Don't even look at her.

Or else, she'll fly away with my heart...

11

VERA

Jack.

Tall, wide-shouldered, grungy hunk with curly black hair and brown eyes that peek out from his glasses.

Jack, who has more definition than a 4k Ultra TV.

The man who shifts into a pumpkin and has a deep voice that fans all kinds of naughty forbidden flames inside of me.

That's the man currently lying on top of me, nibbling at my neck, kissing my shoulder like he needs me more than his next breath. His erection presses into my side, and I arch up to get that oh-so-delicious friction against my lady bits.

If he doesn't peel me out of my clothes soon, I'm going to explode. I *need* him. I need his lips on mine, his hands exploring my heated flesh, his hips thrusting deep inside me.

I moan his name, gripping his tight curls with a plea. He chuckles and pulls my nipple into his mouth. I didn't even realize we were naked, but *thank plasma,* we are. His skin is hot and taut under my questing fingertips. I reach between us to grip his erection, desperate to feel him inside of me.

A startled scream rips out of me when I grip his dick.

It's not made of flesh but a cold, bumpy surface. I pull my hand away, horrified.

I'm holding a zucchini.

Jack isn't above me.

Nope.

There's a massive pumpkin sitting on my chest, its jack-o'-lantern face cackling at me.

What the actual punking pumpkin?

With a jolt, I wake and sit up.

It takes me a few seconds to realize that I'm lying on the couch in the cabin's living room.

I had a sex dream about Jack.

The realization heats my cheeks with embarrassment. Especially since it quickly turned into an absolute nightmare.

Serves me right for lusting after the Pumpkin King who is under my protection.

I seriously doubt Chase Brownsmith would've fuck someone he was meant to protect. More than that, if Director Cooper found out that her broken bat non-agent was going around having almost-dirty dreams about important witnesses, she'd boot me from FUC.

Ousted from FUC because of a fuck is hardly how I want my career in law enforcement to end.

Honestly, I blame Jack for this.

Yesterday, we sat on this very couch and flirted. I put my hand on his *thigh*, inches away from his very human zucchini. When he leaped from the couch and disappeared for the rest of the night, that should've been my clue that he *wasn't* thinking about kissing me.

I almost did.

I was seconds away from kissing Jack before he got out of here like a bat out of hell.

Way to ruin your already precarious career, Vera.

I've got to do something to completely ruin my silly attraction to Jack. Maybe I should start by calling him Norbert. That should do it.

For his part, he better stop wearing those faded jeans that make his ass look more delicious than a juicy steak. And if he doesn't keep his forearms to himself, hidden under his plaid shirt, I'll just have to remind him that this is his home.

Not a strip show.

"Morning, sleepyhead." Jack leans against one of the thick support beams, steaming cup of coffee in hand. His grin is made of sex.

I burrow deeper under the quilt, my face flushing from shame. Does he know? Did I accidentally moan his name out loud while I was dreaming? How am I going to explain *that*?

"Hey, Norbert."

He frowns, his glasses sliding down that sexy nose.

Stop, V. Noses are not sexy. They're functional organs. Nothing more.

"Norbert?" he repeats. "What happened to Jack?" He winks as he hands me the mug of coffee.

Our fingers brush as I accept his kind offering. My already keyed-up organs do a happy flutter, and it takes all of my professionalism to gulp the too-hot coffee.

"I was rude for giving you a nickname. I'll stick to Norbert."

"Why?" he chuckles, settling into the armchair with his own cup of hot bean juice. "I like it. Besides, I *am* a jack-o'-lantern, so the name works."

"Are you asking me to keep calling you Jack?"

His smirk isn't made of sex anymore. Oh, no.

Now it promises orgasms and perfectly dirty kisses.

He takes a swig of his drink and licks his lips to catch a stray drop.

I am a puddle of bat on his couch.

I am a responsible FUC agent. I am not attracted to my charge.

"Did you sleep all right? You look a little pale." His concern is very real and all too sweet. "You should take the bed."

"Not a chance. This is your home. I'm not a guest but an agent on a mission to keep you safe. I can hardly take your bed."

Now maybe if we shared it...

Oh, for the love of echolocation. *Stop.*

"Besides," I quickly add, "I don't want to disrupt your life. It's bad enough you've got to sneak out of here and stay in the lab or in your crops all day."

He chuckles. "I do that whether you're here or not, V. At least now I've got company. I woke up much later today and won't go to bed until sunrise. That way, we can keep the same hours."

I blink at him. "That's hardly a good idea."

Because if we spend more time together, my badge will be on the line.

"It's a great idea," he argues, smiling. "That way, you can take the bed."

"We can alternate," I mumble. "Compromise."

"Great. Love a good compromise. Get dressed. I wanna show you something in the lab."

"Please tell me you didn't scarecrow yourself."

"Nope. This is something for you. I'll be waiting for you downstairs." Jack winks before making his way to the lab.

Do I watch him walk away? Of course I do. There's no way that I can ignore his butt. Or the way his black curls tease the nape of his neck. Everything about the man is delicious.

I really wish I hadn't seen his equipment my first day here. It's one thing to find a man *hot*. It's another to be attracted to him in an *I-have-sex-dreams* way. It's a disaster to know exactly what he's packing.

The dude could do some serious damage with that thing.

Like ruin my career.

———

I took a quick shower, and after much deliberation and a little slip of sanity, I coif my hair. I could lie to myself and say that I only did it because it's easier to go about my day with my elongated bob styled just so.

But the second I slide on my black leggings with mesh material weaving its way around my legs, I know I'm playing a dangerous game. Why I even packed my sexy leggings, I don't know.

I certainly don't have to wear them.

I also don't have to match it with a white crop top.

I'm full of bad choices today, but hopefully, they're all out of my system before I join Jack in the lab.

Ha-ha-fucking-ha.

When I make my way down, back straight and with a solid resolve to be professional, it takes two seconds for that to go right out the window.

Jack is bent over a microscope, and his plaid sleeves are rolled up to his elbows, putting his sinewy muscles on display as he turns the nob on his device. It would be easy enough not to get all aflutter, but *of course* his curls fall over his forehead. He *has* to pucker his lips in concentration. If I didn't know any better, I would think the man is doing this on purpose.

He is trying to make me nutso bananas with lust.

"You're here." He grins and pushes his hair back.

I swallow my tongue. Or maybe it only feels like that because the floor shifts under my feet as his eyes catch mine.

"Come here." He waves me forward and steps away from the microscope. "I wanna show you this. I think you'll really like it."

I am one thirsty bat.

My limbs are glued together with randy goo.

I make my way across the lab, taking breaths that don't quite make it to my brain. Thankfully, I can lean on the countertop as I look down into the scope. It can support me while I watch as two burgundy rings mold together on the thin glass slab.

"What am I seeing?"

"Blood particles."

My stomach lurches, and I jump back. "What?"

Jack's hand settles on my lower back, his fingers grazing the very top of my ass. "Sorry. I should have warned you. I sort of got excited there for a second. I'm trying to break down the nutritional value of blood."

"Why?" My voice is as queasy as my tummy.

"Well, I figure I can try to make something that has all the benefits of blood without actually *being* blood."

Be still my batty heart.

My mouth opens and closes. I'm in shock but also melting because *aw-oh-my-guano-but-this-is-the-sweetest-thing-ever.*

"Wh-what? Why? Why are you doing that?"

"Well, no one should be in physical and emotional

distress once a day to survive. Doesn't seem right to me." He shrugs like it's nothing.

But it's not.

It's... well, it's kind of *everything*.

Jack isn't from a shifter family, and that might be why, for him, my blood aversion isn't some kind of flaw.

It's not something I have to work through or *fix* in myself.

For the first time in a long time—if not *ever*—I don't feel broken. The solution isn't that I need to *get over it* or *toughen up*. Nope. Jack gives me hope that the answer could come from the outside.

And he's willing to fiddle in his lab.

For me.

"Thank you," I whisper. "You really don't have to do that."

"Trust me, V. I really do."

His nickname for me, a simple letter, is so personal, so intimate. No one has ever called me that before. In his deep baritone, the single syllable is an ode to me. It's almost as endearing as his latest experiment.

"I've got a lot of bad shit to make up for while I still can. This is gonna be good for you. Besides, I'm sure there are other bats out there who'd be happy not to drink blood anymore."

He was wrong. Most vampire bats *adored* blood. They thrived on it and on the connection to the old ways, the vampiric ways of the old country. I was the odd bat out, but I wouldn't ruin this moment. It was too special.

I throw my arms around Jack and hug him tight. He's as surprised as I am by the physical contact, but he quickly recovers and wraps his strong arms around my waist, drawing me impossibly closer to him.

"Thank you, Jack," I murmur in his ear before kissing his cheek.

It's a whim. A dangerous one. He stiffens but only for a second. He pulls away slightly, keeping us tied together. One of his hands tips my chin up, and our gazes lock. I can't breathe, but I don't need to when I'm this close to Jack.

"Anything for the batty lady keeping me safe."

For one delicious heartbeat, I believe he'll lean in and kiss me. I lick my lips, tasting my cotton candy lip gloss. I'm so ready for this kiss. I'm pretty sure I've been waiting for it my whole life.

So, of course, it doesn't happen.

Jack's pocket begins to ring, the sound ripping us apart.

12

NORBERT

Saved by the fucking phone.

Did I even *want* to be saved from this moment?

I'm *seconds* away from kissing Vera. My lips tingle in protest as I step away from her and reach for my back pocket.

"Hello, Agent Downer," I say into the device. She's the only person to have this number. It stands to reason she would be the one to call at *the* least convenient time.

It's lucky she did, though, much as it pains me to admit.

"Norbert. How's my favorite whistleblower?"

I wince. "Fine."

"Anything to report?"

I've got blue balls, I'm falling for the agent you sent, and I'm pretty sure I'm one day away from losing my damn mind.

"Nope," I respond. "Everything's good here."

"Nice. That's what we like to hear."

"How about on your side? Did the files help? Are you almost done putting together the charges?"

Downer lives up to her name. "No, Norbert. Sorry.

There's lots of great stuff in what you gave us, but we can't tie any of it to Lisbeth Bannon."

"It's her company," I growl.

"It sort of is, but not on paper. She might give the orders, but she's not the top of the pyramid."

"What does that even mean?"

"You caught a decent fish, but it wasn't the big fish."

My stomach churns. "She's the one who told me to look into the..." My eyes cut to Vera, who is watching me intently, listening to every word. *Shit.* I've got to mince my words. "Lisbeth is in charge," I insist, refusing to bring up the Bloody Doctor's research. "She's the one who's questing hard for this." *There.* Speaking without saying a damn word.

"We have Vitality dead to rights on the toxic waste dump, but it's not gonna do anything. It's too big of a company. They've already paid the fine and agreed to fund part of the cleanup."

My heart sinks. "But they destroyed a full ecosystem."

"Yeah, and we live in a consumer's world where no one gives a fuck if we destroy the planet."

I snort out a dry, sarcastic laugh.

You'd think that the people searching for immortality would give a shit about the state of the environment, that they would treat the *planet* like she's immortal instead of their own personal dumping site.

Where do they think they're going to live if they ever do unlock the secret of eternal life? On the moon? It sure won't be on Earth if they keep treating her like shit.

"So what does this mean? For me? I gave you so much evidence, Downer. Not only with the toxic dumping but with the other experiments, too. It should be enough."

"You're right. It should be. It's not, though. Can't tell you why. The answers are way above my paygrade, and all my superiors have told me is that they need another few weeks to figure out how to deal with this mess."

"A few weeks?" I swallow hard.

Is Downer *really* telling me that Vera will be living with me for months? I can deal with my attraction to her for a few more days—probably. If she has to stay much longer? I don't know how I'll keep away.

Not when she turns those bright hazel eyes on me, smiling with hope and encouragement.

I run a hand across my mouth. "Look, Downer, that's not good enough for me. I can't live with a threat looming over my head for months."

"Maybe you'll think about that next time you decide to play hide-the-pickle with a multi-billion-dollar corporation CEO who wants to live forever."

I can't even argue. Downer is right.

"FUC has agreed to extend your protective custody. If you want, we can alternate the agent. Switch 'em out or whatever."

"Yes." *Wait. That means no more Vera.* "No." *But that means resisting her for months.* "Yeah-no."

"Norbert," Downer warns. "Make up your mind."

"We're good for now."

"Fine. Meanwhile, if you can dig through your files for anything that links Lisbeth Bannon to VH, that'd be great."

I don't bother telling her that I've already given the Cryptozoian Council and FUC everything I have. Downer *knows* that. It's her not-so-subtle way of telling me I am well and truly fucked.

"They won't protect me forever," I grumble.

"You're right. They won't. You might want to start thinking about a change of identity. New home, new name, new career. I'll call you soon to check on things. In the meantime, if you need anything, don't hesitate to call." She ends the connection.

"Well?" Vera nearly hops, waiting for me to reply as I slide the phone into my back pocket. "What's happened? Will the trial be happening any time soon?"

I shake my head before giving her a brief—and abridged—rundown of the news. Vera listens intently, her cute nose scrunching up as I go along.

"None of this makes sense. I'm missing a piece of the puzzle. If Vitality paid the fine and won't get into any more trouble, why do you still need protective custody? It's done, isn't it?"

I don't imagine the sadness rooted in her tone. The corner of Vera's mouth droops down, and I hate it. I want to make her smile again, but I can't. This is the second time she's flat-out asked me for the truth. All of it. If I keep it from her again, there's every chance she'll never forgive me.

For some dumb reason, that's more dangerous than Lisbeth Bannon and everything the shifter could send my way. I weave my fingers with Vera's and lead her to the small garden at the back of the lab. We sit together on the edge of the wooden plant box.

"Okay, so let the record show that I'm slightly freaked out by your silence."

I wince but try to cover it with an uneasy grin. "I've been keeping something from you." My throat bobs like an apple in a barrel.

"Yeah, I kinda figured."

With a sigh that could power my home for a decade, I launch into the whole sordid tale. I leave nothing out. I tell her how Lisbeth seduced me, how my hubris was my undoing. I tell her about the Bloody Doctor and how I've been using her research to find the key to immortality.

To her credit—and to my horror—Vera is quiet as I continue to spew out all of my dark secrets. I've known this woman for four days. Her opinion of me shouldn't matter as much as it does, but there you have it.

I care what Vera Slaski thinks of me.

I want her to think I'm a good man even though I took the work of Sveta Markov, a mass murderer with hundreds of deaths on her hands, and tried to make sense of it. I want Vera to look at me and see *Jack*, the subsistence farmer, and botanist who accidentally turned himself into a pumpkin.

Not the idiot who thought he could fix the world by making the rich and powerful immortal.

"It was about finding a cure for diseases," I repeat for the thousandth time in a minute, hoping against hope that Vera believes me. It's the truth.

But really, why should she take my word for it? We're basically strangers, and I don't have much to recommend me.

"I really wanted to find solutions, but all I did was create a problem. One big fucking problem."

"Did you give Vitality Holdings immortality?"

I shake my head. "No. I don't actually think it's possible. I looked at perennial plants and broke their genome down to the very barest of genes. Even at that, it's not a perfect system. It would mean immortal beings would need to change vessels. Bodies. Cell reconstruction or regeneration is very hard to recreate. They won't get it from plants, anyway. I reached the natural conclusion of my research because... you know, everything has a conclusion. Nothing should be eternal."

Vera stands and begins to pace the length of the lab. She doesn't look my way, keeping her eyes fixed on the floor. A few times, she stops, breathes in deeply with the beginning of a thought, but then deflates and continues pacing.

It's torture, waiting for her reaction.

"Lisbeth Bannon is the CEO of Vitality, right?"

"Yeah, and Vitality Holdings, too. But apparently, she isn't really the top of that company."

"She wouldn't be. It's got to be a front."

"How do you figure?"

"Well, Bannon is hardly the only person chasing immortality. My aunt was all up in that, but she had a bunch of followers. There were blogs dedicated to studying her research. Even when she went nutso bananas and busted out of jail, people praised her work as world-changing. Bannon is probably the mouthpiece for a lot of people who want to live forever."

"Rich, famous, powerful people who don't necessarily want to be associated with a scientist who went mad and killed a bunch of people," I continued for Vera, catching on to her thought process.

"Exactly," Vera agrees. "Downer mentioned they can't bring this up any higher or charge Vitality with anything more serious than the toxic waste, right? What if she's being blocked by someone or some*ones*?"

My eyes pop wide. "You really can't be saying there is a mole in the Cryptozoian Council or FUC."

Vera throws her hands up in the air, defeated. "Well, why not? You're positive you gave them enough evidence against Lisbeth Bannon that they should be able to charge her?"

"I'm not a lawyer. I don't know the law that well."

"I do." She is so invigorated she begins to bounce on her feet. "You need to show me everything you gave Downer."

"Including my research notes?"

"Yup."

"I don't want you to hate me for the shit that I've done."

"Well, I guess we'll cross that bridge if we get to it."

Well, at least that will solve one problem. Vera will despise me, and my attraction to her will be moot.

IT TAKES hours for Vera to read through everything I shared with the Cryptozoian Council.

It's near sunrise by the time she pushes away from the old computer. She arches her back before bending at the waist, letting her fingertips brush the floor. I try not to look at the curve of her lush ass. I fail. Vera's hips flare out like a perfect hourglass that makes my mouth water. Here we are, in a tense and uncertain junction, and I'm ogling her.

You're an ass, Jack.

"And? What's the verdict, counselor?"

Vera continues to stretch, throwing an arm over her shoulder, arching into the movement as if she were presenting her breasts to me. The thin material of her shirt stretches over her chest while her crop top inches dangerously high, giving me a quick peek at her bra.

Trouser zucchinis are in season, apparently.

"Well, I honestly have to agree with Downer on this one. Lisbeth Bannon is listed as the CEO in absentia. She isn't the one pulling strings. She's a puppet. Probably a fancy puppet like a possessed ventriloquist doll, but there's someone with their hand up her ass." She cringes. "Sorry for the bad analogy. My brain is a little bit fried from all that reading. I haven't read that much since law school."

"It was quite the visual." But what did that make *me*? I was the string puppet to a ventriloquist doll?

Double damn with a side of fuck.

"Unless we got access to all kinds of financial information, it would be impossible to figure out who Bannon is working for. Even at that, if she really is the mouthpiece for the rich and powerful, they'll have all of that intel buried in offshore accounts and all kinds of shady shit."

Wrecked like a carriage after midnight, I slouch down onto the wooden plant box. "What does this mean? What do we do?"

Vera slides down beside me. "Honestly? I've got no idea. Full disclosure? I'm not a full agent yet."

It's my turn to jump to my feet.

"Director Cooper is keeping my badge until I can ingest blood like a normal vampire bat. I'm not as connected as a *real* agent would be. I don't think Alyce expected this to be so complicated. On the surface, this really was just some glorified babysitting job."

"Sorry."

"Don't be. You were played, and then you tried to make it right. Now we need to evaluate our next course of action. We also need to figure out why Director Cooper didn't have all of this information from Downer. I know she and Erhart Know, the rep for the Cryptozoian Council don't exactly get along, but this is weird. What's Downer's plan for us?"

"Downer wants us to stay here for weeks. Months maybe, while they figure their shit out."

"Right. Maybe we can help them along with that. Can you do more digging from here?"

"Not really," I answer. Her shoulders deflate slightly. "I only have internet for a few hours every night, and it's not super reliable."

"Damn. If we could do more digging here, at least we could have hope of finding *something*. We can't trust anyone right now. I would reach out to Jessie Cyngclair at FUC. She's the tech pro and swan shifter. I *know* she's one of the good guys, but it's something I'd want to discuss in person. I don't know that I trust any phone lines right now. Not to mention, we're stuck here. It's not a secure location. Not anymore, anyway. If we don't know who to trust, we have to assume this place is compromised. Downer would have told her superiors. Director Cooper knows, which means others might as well. Hell, maybe I was followed."

"We can't be naive and think Bannon didn't figure out my location, either."

"Then there's that, yeah."

I push the heels of my palms into my eyes, taking deep breaths. "I fucked this up royally."

"If it wasn't you, it would be someone else. Maybe someone who wouldn't have blown the whistle. No use playing *what-if*. We need a game plan."

"I'm all ears."

"I have an idea. It's bad and dangerous, but it might be our only shot at rooting out any potential moles all the while figuring out who Lisbeth Bannon represents."

"Okay?"

"We have to go on the run."

I still. "On the run." I test the words on my tongue, but I don't like them. "That does sound pretty perilous."

"Well, we wouldn't be on the run or in the wilderness for long. I think we should make our way over to my cousin Mila's place."

"The Bloody Doctor's daughter?"

"Yeah. She and her husband, T-Bone, are both FUC agents, but I trust them with my life. The second Mila learns that her mother's research is being used by other people, she'll want to be involved. She'll want to stop it as much as we do."

"And you trust this cousin?"

"She's as batty as they come, but yeah. I trust her. If someone is using her mother's research *again*, she'll want to know and help us stop it. That's a guarantee."

I fill my lungs until they ache. I hate leaving the cabin and my crops. I'm not a fan of the big wide world. Not to mention the fact that I have zero defensive skills. I turn into a huge pumpkin when I'm threatened.

Visions of Vera running through the forest holding a massive gourd while being chased by Lisbeth makes me shudder.

"Give me twenty-four hours."

"Twenty-four hours," Vera agrees.

13

VERA

The preparations for our escape are going as well as can be expected.

Jack is reluctant to leave his farm behind. If he didn't give his crops constant attention, he might lose them all. He wouldn't have much—or any—food when he returns.

If he returns.

There's no way of knowing how this plays out.

Lose your crop, or lose your life.

That's not exactly the best choice. I feel for the dude. I really do. It has *nothing* to do with how he makes me feel.

As I pack up some supplies for us, the very last thing on my mind should be Jack. I can't help myself. As hard as it was to share a small one-bedroom cabin with the man, it'll be impossibly harder to share a tent with him as we hike our way back to civilization.

We considered taking the armored car that I drove here, but there's risk there. FUC has trackers in all of its vehicles. We can't take any chances and take an easily traceable car. We can't take the chance that there *is* a mole in FUC.

That would completely defeat the purpose of going on the lam.

When Jack requested twenty-four hours before we depart, I don't know what I expected him to do. I thought he needed time to wrap his head around leaving home.

Not so much.

He hasn't left the lab for more than ten minutes at a time. Every time he surfaces, I ask if he's okay, if he needs help. He assures me he doesn't, grabs a protein bar, and returns to his lair. I don't really know what he's doing down there, but I'm assuming it has to do with the straw he hauled in earlier this evening.

The only time I almost crept down to see how he was doing was when the scent of burning sugar hit my nostrils, but he rushed up the stairs to tell me that all was well, grabbed the fire extinguisher from under the kitchen sink, and vanished again.

That was about three hours ago.

It's late now.

Late enough that the sun will be rising soon. I'm *starving* enough to gnaw on some raw veggies as I continue to stir the stew I've made for us. Cooking vegetarian isn't as easy as throwing a bunch of vegetables into a dish and calling it a day.

The human body needs protein—loads of it—to function properly. I threw all kinds of beans and gourds into the stew, making it as hearty and filling as I can.

Not that I know what I'm doing, really. I'm following a recipe in one of Jack's cooking books, but I've tweaked it to use the ingredients the sexy subsistence farmer has on hand.

Jack's footsteps echo up the staircase, and he emerges, plaid shirt discarded, his white tee rumpled and filthy. Even his gray jeans are a right mess. "Hey," he sighs, his voice rough and tired.

"You should go take a nice long shower before you pass out on your feet. Dinner is almost ready."

"Yeah. Thanks. Good idea." He reaches back and pulls his shirt off in one smooth motion that has my nether regions fluttering.

I ogle because of *course* I do. I am mesmerized by the muscles on his back as he walks by. How does the body's musculature work? I've got no clue, but I'd love to understand how his back undulates with power and grace as he stalks away.

The sound of the shower kicking on snaps me out of my temporary hypnosis. I return to the kitchen and busy myself over pots and pans as I do my level best *not* to imagine Jack in the shower.

Why is that, every time the dude bathes, I imagine what it would be like to be a total creeper and watch? Standing there, stirring a stew over the stovetop, picturing Jack stroking his impressive hardware isn't helpful.

It's *definitely* not professional.

I like rules. I love to follow them. I *never* break them.

Yes, I sort of fibbed about the whole blood thing, but no one thought to ask, and I thought I could get over it.

This is different. I can't exactly help the way Jack makes me feel. I'm a hopeful, giddy mess because I know there's something between us. Or there could be if our circumstances weren't so messed up.

By the time the water turns off, I've overcooked dinner, drooled enough to power a dam, and made myself way too horny for a trek through the wild. I'm not here to obsess over Jack but to get one up on an evil shifter corporation seeking immortality.

I give my loins a talking-to.

Listen lady, Jack isn't for us. He is our charge, and he is in some serious trouble. Complicating things with a roll in the pumpkin patch is not a good idea.

There.

That should do it.

I roll my shoulders back and decide that my silly attraction to Jack can—and will—be totally ignored until it no longer exists.

Like my blood aversion.

I super have this under control.

That goes out the window *real fucking* fast. The bathroom door swings open, and there he stands, in all his wet and naked glory. A brown towel is wrapped around his trim waist, but it leaves very little to the imagination.

Especially an imagination that's *seen* the goods and dreamed about them every night since.

"Forgot to grab clean clothes," he explains, blushing deep red. He scurries to the bedroom, leaving wet footprints behind.

I'm not entirely sure Jack didn't do that to torture me or something. Maybe he's trying to tease me to death. Is that a thing? It has to be.

Here lies Vera Slaski, slain by her overeager and lonely loins.

"Sorry about that." Jack is fully clothed, and I swear to the good lords of birth control, my vagina weeps.

"All good." My voice is way too high-pitched and cheery. Jack would see a shade of red as-of-yet undiscovered by the human eye if he saw my face.

I load a plate down with mashed potatoes and top it with a few massive scoops of stew before placing it on the kitchen table. It smells really good if I do say so myself. Jack settles at his seat and digs in. He shovels a huge bite into his mouth and winces.

"Is it bad?" I wince.

He shakes his head, gobbling up some more. "No. So good. Really hot, but I'm too starved to wait. Thanks for this." He wipes his mouth on the back of his hand, his handsome face turning sheepish. "Sorry for the whole savage act. I didn't realize how hungry I was until I ate."

"It's fine. You've been in the lab for a while. I needed *something* to do, or I was gonna go batty. Maybe cool your jets, Jack." I giggle as he devours the rest of his plate and gets up to grab some more. "But I'm happy it's edible. Especially since it may very well be our last warm meal before we head out tomorrow."

"That reminds me..." Jack settles at the table. "We need to find a solution for your sun allergy if we aren't taking the car."

"I've mapped out our journey. We're going to be in the woods for two nights."

"That means two full days of sun you need to avoid. It seems like too big a risk. I've been thinking... What if we drive the car in the *opposite* direction? Ditch it. Buy a clunker somewhere. It seriously reduces our travel time and your risk of sun exposure."

I ponder this. "It sort of goes against all of my training."

"I kinda think that this whole situation isn't exactly your run-of-the-mill mission."

You're telling me.

I doubt other agents are out there, falling wingtips over tail for their charges. Not that I'm admitting that I've developed any sort of feelings for Jack in seven days.

That would be *ridiculous.*

As ridiculous as a grown man shifting into a pumpkin every time he's threatened.

"I'd prefer we didn't take any chances with your health. What happens if you catch some sun?"

"I explode into a pile of ash," I deadpan.

His fork stops halfway to his mouth. "You're hilarious." He rolls his eyes. "For real, V. Be honest. Our plan can't only factor in the outward danger. We also need to take our limitations into consideration. And that's not to say only your sun allergy. We need to be smart about this. If we're out in the wild, hiking up to your cousin's place, and we get attacked? I'll literally turn into a useless gourd. Your bat can't carry me, and you can't defend yourself *and* my orange ass all at once."

His tush is not orange, though I'm willing to bet it's just as firm as a ripe gourd.

"I think," Jack goes on, completely oblivious to the impact he has on me, "our best bet is taking the car."

It takes a few minutes for my brain to catch up with the conversation. I'm not sure it's a good idea, but I don't want to shoot it down without thinking about it. I grab my empty bowl and bring it to the sink as I mull it all over.

Jack's right, of course. If we were set upon and he turns into a pumpkin, the odds are stacked against us. Does it make me a bad agent—or *almost* agent—that I want to take his plan into consideration? Shouldn't I have all of the answers?

I rinse my bowl and begin clearing away the dishes.

Jack is quick to join me. "I can feel you thinking."

"Impossible."

"I think that hearing thoughts' echolocation might be my superpower." He winks.

"That's not a thing."

He shrugs. "No, but I can tell from the small pucker right here"—he brushes his fingers along my brow—"you're thinking real hard."

His skin on mine set off sparklers in my brain. The touch might be chaste, but it's intimate.

That's the only explanation for why my hands end up on his shoulders, inching up to settle at the back of his neck.

"Thanks for dinner." His voice caresses my face.

"You're welcome," is what I *think* I say.

I'm not too sure if I actually open my mouth to speak because, the next second, my lips are pressed to his in a tender kiss. Jack's arms wrap around my waist, holding me close to him. His lips are soft but demanding as he takes control of the embrace.

Right there, in the small kitchen of a one-bedroom cabin, I devour Dr. Norbert *Jack* Palomer's face like I need it more than my next breath.

One of his hands finds its way to my hair, and the other cups my ass. He presses me into him, making it pretty damn clear that this kiss is heated.

It could definitely lead to something more.

I tense as I remember who he is and, more to the point, who I am and why I'm here.

Good agents don't check out their charges. If Director Cooper could see me now, my aversion to blood would be the least of my worries.

Rules and control, Vera. Rules. And. Control.

"V," he whispers against my mouth. He doesn't say anything more but presses his lips to mine again in a sweet kiss, bookending our make-out session with something straight out of an afterschool special.

"I should continue the cleanup."

I blurt out the words as I push away from him. The second I leave his arms I miss him. I want more of him.

Hell, I want all of him.

My responsibilities as an agent and my desires as a woman clash more than lipstick on a bat.

I am in deep *guano*.

14

NORBERT

Vera nervously brushes her hair back as she pushes away from me.

Damn, damn, double damn.

I should not have kissed her, but I don't want to regret the best kiss of my life.

I understand I crossed a line, but I couldn't help myself. Seems that Vera was into it herself until her brain caught up with her.

Needing to reconnect with her and make up for mauling her after she made me such a good meal, I take her hand in mine and tug her toward the door. "Come with me. I wanna show you what I've been working on."

I bound down the steps, pulling Vera behind me. I pull out a stool for her and help her settle on it before grabbing the prototype. The small canister of blood Director Cooper sent has been washed and sanitized and emptied of the stuff that makes Vera ill.

I replaced it with my own creation.

"This is only a trial. It will need tweaking, but it was the best I could do in such a short amount of time." I open the receptacle and hand it over to her. "Go on. Take a sip."

Vera arches a brow at me. "Am I supposed to trust the man who accidentally turned himself into a pumpkin?" Her teasing smirk goes straight to my heart.

"That's a fair point. But trust me, this is gonna be wonderful."

"Are you going to tell me what this is first?"

I uncap the container with a grin and take a sniff from it before offering her the chance to do the same. "And?" I ask. "Any adverse feelings?"

She shakes her head. "Should I have a bad reaction?"

My smile widens. "That's a blood substitute. Or at least, what I *hope* can be a blood substitute. Taste it."

Vera pales, but the apples of her cheeks become bright like cherries. "What if I get sick? Or pass out?"

"Then I'll take care of you. I promise I did the very best I could to make this as palatable as possible. I've had some, and I'm still standing."

Warily, Vera takes hold of the canister and brings it to her nose. She gives it a couple of sniffs and twirls it, taking another whiff. "It doesn't *smell* like blood. I don't feel faint." Slowly, as if she were about to drink poison, Vera brings it to her lips and takes a cursory sip.

"Why does it taste like cotton candy?"

Heat burns my cheeks.

Because that's what you smell like. Because that's what your kisses taste like.

"I wanted it to have a pleasant aftertaste," I answer with a shrug.

"This definitely explains the smell of burning sugar."

"Yeah, let's not talk about that. Production was interesting. Let's leave it at that."

"You shouldn't have done this," she whispers. "Though I'm not sure I've ever had someone give me a gift so sweet and meaningful. But you should've been focusing on *your* situation, Pumpkin King."

She's not wrong, but I can't help it. Somehow, making sure Vera is safe and can survive easily became my priority.

Because that's super normal when you've known a woman for seven nights.

Only, it hasn't just been seven nights. Not really. It's not like we're meeting in the real world, going out on a couple of dates here and there. All of our time is spent together, and we're literally the only person around. That's not to say I wouldn't have wanted to impress Vera if we met under different circumstances.

I *know*—down to the very core of me—that Vera would have caught my eye and my interest no matter where or how we met.

"What am I gonna do if you turn into a gourd out there? Kiss you with my magic cotton candy lips?"

She thinks she means because of the blood.

I mean her lip gloss.

I can't help it. My hand moves of its own volition to tuck a strand of her hair behind her ear. She leans forward, her breath hitching along.

"Your kiss would definitely have some magical qualities. Fairy tale stuff, for sure." And because I'm a lot cheesy and a little into her, I brush a kiss on her smile.

I'm not prepared for the sheer magnitude of the desire that hits me. Vera sighs into my mouth, her hands pressing against my chest as she arches up to kiss me.

A real kiss.

One that has her standing from the stool to pin herself to

me. Her lips on mine, moving to the same rhythm. Her hands on me, mine gripping her ass to pull her into me.

I was right. *This is a fairy tale* kind of kiss. It erases everything for my mind except Vera Slaski, bat shifter, lawyer, agent, cute as a button, hot as sin, and everything in between.

She came here to protect me from the outside world, but she's why I want to rejoin it.

I want to take her out on proper dates. I want to hold her hand as we walk down the street. I want to lay her down and show her how good it could be between us.

So much for never trusting another person ever again.

"This is really sweet, Jack." The warm brown of her eyes melts into whirlpools of chocolate, pulling me closer to her with the force of a vortex. Vera stands on the tips of her toes and kisses my cheek. "Thank you."

She's *right* there. So close to me. Vera doesn't want to let me go any more than I want to let her go.

I know Lisbeth Bannon really fucked me over. Shit, she might have very well ruined my life if it hadn't brought me to this exact moment. If Lisbeth hadn't used me for her own gain, then I never would have blown the whistle on Vitality. I never would have reached out to Val Downer.

I never would have met Vera Slaski.

A world without the batty lady seems so dull and colorless.

Now that I know this woman exists, I don't want to ever forget that her hazel gaze shines amber when the light hits it just right. I want to memorize the Cupid bow of her lips, the sweet scent of cotton candy.

If I had to get my ass handed to me by Lisbeth Bannon to meet Vera Slaski, I would do it all over again. That's saying something.

"I'll have to make more of it. Probably tweak it to maximize its nutritional value, but at least it's a good start."

"Well, when I was growing up, Raya used to talk about the powerful satiated feeling she had after drinking blood. I never had that because I was too busy feeling sick. I feel pretty satisfied right now. That's a good sign. Though, that very well could be because of the kiss."

Vera smacks a hand over her mouth, surprised by her own words.

Pleased and every bit victorious, I chuckle. "It could be. I'm pretty *satisfied* with that, too." *Though I could go for more.* A quick glance at the clock on the wall tells me it's nearly time for us to get to bed.

Separately.

Right?

I definitely *shouldn't* push my luck and try to take things further with Vera. Nope. It would be a bad idea.

"I should go back upstairs and finish packing and cleaning up the kitchen."

"I'll help. I've done enough science experiments today."

"I really can't complain about that. I really thought you were down here trying to find a solution to the pumpkin thing. Not making a blood substitute for me."

I shrug. "I've been working on the pumpkin situation since it happened. I've got a few things up my sleeve. Besides, it always helps me to work on a different project while I let things simmer in my brain. It's like taking a shower or gardening and having some brilliant ideas pop in randomly. The answer comes when your mind is busy doing something else."

"I'm very grateful, Jack. It really was the sweetest thing anyone has ever done for me."

I smirk, my heart expanding big and wide in my chest. "You're very welcome."

"Now, you stay down here and try to find a way to not explode into a pumpkin." She arches a brow at me, giving me a stern look that makes me want to throw her over my shoulder and bring her to bed. "If you succeed in your experiment, there might be more of this." Vera kisses me softly before retreating up the stairs.

There will never be a greater motivator than a kiss from Vera Slaski.

15

NORBERT

By the time I climb the stairs up to the cabin, I'm exhausted.

I made a bit of progress.

Enough to inject myself with it.

Is it safe? No.

Do I know what will happen? No.

But I *have* to try something.

The very last thing I want is for us to be attacked and Vera to be all alone. She isn't a defenseless creature. She is a capable bat. She wouldn't be an agent—sort of—if she weren't. It's bullshit that she was kept from graduating because of her blood aversion, but I don't make the rules. All I can do for her is help her however I can.

That's creating the blood alternative.

Two large backpacks are propped up against the wall by the entrance. A small, rectangular orange bag holds the wee two-person tent.

It's been difficult enough on my sanity to have the delectable Vera in my space this past week. I can't even imagine how difficult it'll be to share a tent.

Not that I want us to be attacked or anything, but it

would be that much easier to resist her if we were running for our lives.

Vera sits on the couch, feet tucked under her, book clutched in her hand. Her brown hair is down and frames her face perfectly. The loose red tank droops low, giving me a teasing glimpse of all the things I shouldn't want. Her white sleep shorts are patterned over with little red hearts. One of those is mine.

"And? How did it go?"

"It went," I answer, taking a seat beside her.

"Did you find a solution?"

"Time will tell."

She frowns, her lips pulling into a pout I want to kiss. "I really wish you would have focused on yourself instead of my dumb blood thing."

"It's not a dumb blood thing," I assure her, cupping her knee to give it a comforting squeeze. I mean for the gesture to be sweet, but my dick doesn't understand the friendly touch. I ignore it as best I can. "You've been more than brave about your aversion to blood your whole life. I'm happy to help. Really. It's *not* dumb."

Vera shrugs and drops her book onto the coffee table. "It sure set me apart."

"That's not a bad thing. Besides, if you were all down with the blood, you wouldn't be here."

Her eyes catch mine, flitting from left to right as she tries to decipher my meaning. For a second, I think she'll flirt back. Help a fellow out.

She doesn't.

She folds her knees up to her chin, curling herself into a tiny ball of delicious Vera. "We'll be ready to go as soon as we wake up," she explains. "I think we should get to bed now. We'll wake up when the sun is still up, but at least we can hit the road. The sooner we get to Mila's place, the better."

"I still think we should take the car." I really don't like the idea of her out there, at the mercy of the sun. I didn't create a blood alternative only to have Vera die because of her sun allergy. "You really haven't considered it?"

She shakes her head. "If there *is* a mole in FUC or even the Cryptozoian Council, I don't want to be tracked."

"Fine. But that means we share the bed tonight." Without preamble, I scoop her into my arms.

Vera squeaks and squirms as I walk us to the bedroom. "What the hell do you think you're doing?"

"If we're going to sleep in a tent for the next two nights, if you insist on putting yourself in direct contact with the sun, well then, you need to have at least one decent night's sleep in a bed. I insist."

"Apparently," she grumbles when I lay her down on my pillow.

She sits up and crosses her arms. "You don't play fair. You can't just *manhandle* me like that." Her eyes sparkle with amber and gold. Her nostrils flare with something. Passion? Desire?

Her nipples peeking through the thin material of her tank are answer enough.

A burning need to tease the nubs with my tongue makes my already interested cock perk up with more interest.

"You really think we should share a bed tonight?"

"Yup." I take off my tee and throw it into the laundry basket. I turn to face her, and Vera's pupils dilate as she takes in my bare chest. "It's happening. We can build a wall of pillows between us if that'll make you more comfortable."

"Okay." She doesn't move, her gaze hooked onto mine.

"Okay," I repeat, standing there in nothing but a pair of jeans that put my erection on display.

She peeks down, and her breath hitches when she notices the impact she has on me. "Maybe this is a bad idea."

Vera's words don't match her actions. She pounces off the bed and leaps into my arms. Her lips find mine as she holds on to my shoulders. Stunned but oh-so-pleased, I wrap my arms around her and lift her off the ground. Her legs wrap around my waist, and I pin her to me by cupping her ass. My tongue delves into her mouth. Cotton candy, want, and need explode through my senses, leaving me dizzy and moaning into the kiss.

I lay her down onto the bed and cover her body with mine, quick to return my lips to hers. Her fingers dig into my nape as she explores my mouth, her hips clear off the bed to grind against my erection. My hand travels up her shirt, savoring the soft skin of her stomach, pebbling under my touch. I graze her nipple with my thumb before rolling it between my fingers. Vera nips at my lower lip in answer.

"Jack," she moans, arching her hips toward me.

"V," I whisper in her ear. "What are we doing here?"

"I don't know." Her eyes are pools of dark, warm honey, pulling me, gluing me to her.

I don't want to be anywhere else than right here.

"I want you," rumbles out of me, heavy with truth and lust and a longing so profound it has a vise-grip on my spine.

"Ditto."

No sooner is the word out of her mouth than I take her lips with mine, nipping at the lower one, exploring her mouth, letting our tongues melt together. Her hand fumbles with my pants while mine peel her out of her sleep shorts. Thankfully, they slide right off, giving me plenty of time to get rid of her top, leaving a very bare, very naked Vera on my bed.

There's never been a lovelier sight.

I want to relish this moment and remember it forever. Her look of sheer desire and raw passion nearly sets me aflame.

"You want this?" I ask, my voice rough.

"Yes. I want *you.*"

Thank fuck. I don't know if I speak the words or think them because I'm too concerned with having a taste of Vera. Her bent knees grip my waist as I lower myself down her body.

"What are you doing? Get back here and kiss me," she huffs.

Oh, I'll kiss you all right.

My lips settle right onto the apex of her thighs with a full open-mouth kiss. Her hips lift from the bed as she chases the sensation.

Saucy bat.

I run my tongue over the tight bundle of nerves over and over again before sucking it into my mouth. Vera's pants spur me on, and soon, her legs tremble at my sides. She purrs my name, pleading for that sweet release. I slowly slip a finger inside her heat, quickly followed by another one.

That's all it takes.

Vera cries out, grinding against me to squeeze every ounce of pleasure from the moment. I continue to lap at her center, my gaze fixed on her blissed-out face.

She is, without a doubt, the loveliest woman I've ever seen.

"That... you..." She tries to speak but gives up, lying back against the pillows with a giggle. "I need a second before we go further."

"We don't have to." I make my way up and hover over her. The tip of my erection brushes against her skin, weeping for attention.

"Uh, yeah. We really do."

I chuckle. "My oral skills not enough for you?"

"Not sure it would ever be enough," she responds before surprising the hell out of me and using her toned thighs and arms to spin us around. Vera straddles me, pinning me to the bed, her soft brown hair a halo around us. "Please tell me you've got protection somewhere in this cabin."

I wince because I do. A leftover box of condoms from my time with Lisbeth, but that doesn't matter. If I can empty the box with Vera, then it'll have been worth it. I reach over to the bedside table and grab one. Vera leans over me, kissing me sweetly to grab it from my hand. I watch, riveted and fascinated, as she rips the wrapper and rolls the condom onto my erection.

It shouldn't be sexy to watch her do that, but it is. Vera looks down at me with her hazel eyes burning for me. That's heady as hell.

"You ready?" she coos, pumping my girth with a naughty smirk.

"Vera," is all I'm able to say.

She lines us up and eases me in. She takes all the time in the world to lower down onto my length, prolonging the moment in the most amazing torture. When I'm finally encased in her wet heat, she tilts her hips forward, clenches her walls around me, and rolls her hips.

By all the good gods of creation.

The pleasure surges up my spine, a vise closing around my balls. If she does that again, I'll embarrass myself.

Vera places her hands on my chest for leverage as she continues to ride me. I grip her hips, letting her drive. For now, at least. Her breasts hover over my mouth, and I tug her down to circle the nub with my tongue. She bucks against me with a gasp. I repeat the gesture before sucking hard, letting my teeth graze it. I lick a line across her chest to give the other nipple the same attention.

Vera is a mewling vixen above me, taking me for everything she wants, everything she needs.

Her back arches back as she pushes away from my chest. Her eyes hook on mine, and I see it right about the same time as I feel it. Her core grips me hard, and her pace increases. She gasps, and heat floods me. Vera cries my name as she chases her release.

I'm not far behind.

There's no chance I can last much longer after that. I buck off the bed, pistoning my hips to meet her. My hands tighten on her hips, and I hold her there as I go over the edge, bellowing her name.

It takes me a few moments to move again. When my legs start being legs again, I run to the bathroom to discard the condom and dive back into bed, nestling Vera into my side.

This might have been ill-advised.

Shit, it might even end in my heart breaking.

But if Vera would be willing, I'd give this thing between a chance.

16

VERA

Sweet flying mammal, that was amazing.

So damn good and so damn unexpected that I'm not entirely sure what to do. I don't really want to move. I want to stay right here, lying in Jack's arms, listening to his heartbeat settle after our tryst.

"I guess we ended up sharing the bed after all," Jack whispers before kissing my shoulder.

Naked and sprawled, intertwined and drunk on the afterglow, I giggle. "It seems that way, yes."

"You're not going back to the couch after that, Vera. You're staying right here."

"You better believe it," I shoot back with a snort. "This bed is so damn comfortable. I might never leave. Think we can drag it with us on our trek?"

He chuckles, the sound smooth and warm. "Anything you want, V."

Jack is being funny.

Yet, there is something else. It's heavy like he means something more. Something profound.

Get it together, V. You've known the dude a week. You've kissed a couple of times and had sex once. *This is hardly the greatest love story ever told.*

A small voice in the back of my mind argues softly with an *it could be.*

"Do you snore?" Jack asks. "Should I be prepared for some seriously bad sleeping habits?"

I pinch his side, and he laughs, holding me tighter. "I'm a great sleeper, but we can't stay in bed yet. We still need to prepare some last-minute stuff. We gotta be ready to go as soon as we wake up."

"One more minute," he murmurs, making me shiver. He nestles his head in my hair, sniffing me. "You smell so damn good. One more minute."

"Fine," I relent dramatically with an eye roll, but really, I don't want to go anywhere. I want to soak in this moment for as long as we possibly can. "One more, but then it's up and work time."

"Yes, Agent Slasky."

"Oh, call me that again. It was super sexy."

Jack brushes the shell of my ear with his lips. "Agent. Slaski." His breath flutters against my skin, and I swear I'm ready for round two.

"You're an evil, tempting man, Jack."

"I do my best," he chuckles, making my body zing all over again.

A loud and echoing *bang* makes the walls of the cabin shake and quiver. I jump out of bed, naked as the day I was born, in a defensive stance.

"Stay behind me," I order Jack.

He's already slipping on his boxers and stalking toward the door. "It's probably the damn squirrels. They likely made on of the rakes fall. They do it all the time."

"Jack," I hiss. "If you go Full Gourd on me, I swear..."

I don't have the time to finish my thought. Jack swings the door open, and there stand three people, dressed in black from head to toe, their faces covered by balaclavas.

Shit shit shit. Jack is about to turn veg on me.

"Who do you think you are, busting into my ho—" His sentence dies down as one of the intruders strikes out at him.

Jack dodges, and I lunge, ready to strike. It takes very little time for my human body to shrink down to my bat. I might be an itty-bitty thing, but I can do lots of damage.

As a vampire bat, I've got teeth and claws for days. I slash at one of the interlopers, slicing through his mask. The smell of blood immediately hits me, but I don't focus on it.

Nope.

I keep repeating to myself over and over again that Jack is about to be one defenseless creature. I need to get the upper hand and fast.

Protect Jack is my only rational thought.

I fly up to the ceiling, only to dive down again, incisors at the ready. My batty gut churns at the thought of tasting blood, but again, I push the thought away, thinking only of Jack.

I latch onto one of our attackers, my teeth digging deep. I'm not careful, not like when I'm forced to feed on other mammals. I rip the sensitive skin of the neck like a rabid hound. I even use my legs to gash and slice.

Hot, disgusting blood oozes.

It's a lot.

My brain and body want to revolt, but I'll do that later.

I'll need about a gallon of mouth wash and another of antacid to get over *that*.

I fly up to the ceiling, hooking my claws into the wall. From the vantage point, I spot one of the prowlers helping the one I've wounded while the third just stands there, staring down at an enormous orange gourd.

Wait. Why would a trespasser be immobile right now?

Horrified — and surprised as hell — I spot Jack.

I shout his name, but it comes out like a loud squeak. I dive down toward him, my poor, sweet, defenseless Pumpkin King. But before the goon can get the jump on him, the large gourd begins to rattle and vibrate.

I've seen this happen before.

Jack is about to blow.

I hold my breath and wait for a very naked Jack to appear.

That's not what happens.

The pumpkin wobbles to and fro as if it were sitting on hydraulic limbs. The man staggers back, equal parts confused and terrified. It's not every day you see a grown human turn into a pumpkin before said vegetation begins to move of its own accord.

The jack-o'-lantern, with an actual face carved onto its surface, *sprouts two stubby legs.* As the gourd continues to gain height, the legs grow and grow and grow some more. It takes me a minute to realize that the pumpkin has also grown arms.

Jack is no longer a pumpkin.

He's a scarecrow with a jack-o'-lantern for a head.

I. Am. Freaked. The. Fuck. Out.

He isn't too steady on his legs but staggers forward. The remaining intruder whimpers and edges back, making the shape of the cross with both of his index fingers.

I want to laugh, but I get it.

It's a downright shocking sight to see.

The two others, still trying to staunch the bleeding, notice Jack. The injured one slips to the floor, holding on to his neck, while the other grabs for a gun. He shoots directly at Jack, and I swoop down, claws at the ready. I slash at the gunman's forehead, barely managing to slice through the material of his balaclava. A quick peek at Jack to make sure he's okay has my wings sputtering mid-flight.

The gun didn't shoot bullets. Nope. Huge tranquilizer darts stick out of Jack's straw chest, leaving me no doubt that Jack hauled hay into the lab to make himself into a scarecrow.

I really hope he can change back.

At the very least, Jack doesn't seem to be the least bit affected by the tranquilizer. He keeps advancing toward our foe, swiping long hands made of straw. He looks like something right out of a nightmare or a horror movie, but I can't make myself look away.

His body—if I can call it that—makes no sense.

The straw of his limbs and torso are woven together like one giant poppet with a pumpkin sitting atop a neck like a crown.

I'd bet my left incisor that if he had spent more time on his formula than on making a blood alternative for me, he would have figured out a way to dress his scarecrow somehow.

My man is brilliant.

Only, he isn't my man, and this is certainly not the time to be thinking about what the sex meant.

I flap my wings a few times and fly by his line of vision, making sure to catch his attention. He makes a terrible groaning sound, and all I can do is hope he follows. The interlopers, stunned and scared that their weapons are not working on the massive scarecrow, scamper out of his way. The incapacitated one on the floor whimpers and rolls out of Jack's way.

I land on one of the bags I packed and flutter my wings.

Please understand me. Pick up this bag. It has some clothes for our naked asses.

"They're gonna get away," one of the men shouts.

"Yeah, well, *you* go after 'em."

"Not a chance," comes the answer. "Did you see? That's too freaky for my pay grade."

With strange and stunted movements, Jack picks up the bag, swings it over his shoulder, and it flies across the room before crashing against the wall. Without being prompted —*thank blood bags for sentient beings*—he picks up the second one and lumbers out the door and down the steps.

He goes to the passenger side of the vehicle and nearly rips the door off its hinges before throwing the bag into the backseat and plopping onto the seat. His head falls and rolls at his feet, but I don't have time to deal with that.

I need to get us *out* before the idiot goons wise up. I shift back into my human form, naked once again, and hop into the car. I scan my thumb against the small biometric pad in the dash. It's a good thing to have for shifter agents. When we take our human form, we're nude with no pockets or nook or cranny for our keys. The fingerprint key is... well, key.

The armored car roars to life, and I floor it.

17

VERA

I clutch the steering wheel with all my might to keep the panic at bay, but really, the last thirty minutes of my life have been a little bit intense.

Amazing sex with a hot farming scientist.

Cute post-coital cuddling.

Three intruders barging in.

Yup. This is definitely *not* a regular mission and *definitely not* how I planned on leaving the cabin.

On the seat next to me, the straw scarecrow slowly starts to lose shape, basically melting into a pile of hay.

"If you go and explode on me right now, Jack Palomer, I'm gonna be so pissed."

I have no idea what happens when Jack shifts back into his body. The only time I saw it happen, there was pumpkin goo everywhere in the lab.

As I try to navigate the massive SUV down the narrow and overrun dirt road, I take quick glances at the gourd. Slowly, it begins to vibrate.

"Do. Not. Splat," I warn.

But he has no real control over it. It's not like humans

are *supposed* to morph into vegetation. It's enough of an oddity that I turn into a bat the size of a child's teacup. But this?

Well, it defies all nature *and* logic.

"Where do your organs even go?" I ask aloud, probably to find something to think about other than the impending pumpkin bath I'm about to take.

A quick glance at the rearview mirror, and it's clear. Whatever the goons are doing, they aren't following us.

Weird.

At least it gives me a good idea. I slam on the brake, leap out of the car, run around the front, and grab hold of Jack.

It's a really good thing this man has already seen me naked.

I lay the pumpkin down on the forest ground and wave my hand over him. "Let's go. Be human."

It shakes and vibrates, but nothing happens.

I kneel by it and give the gourd a peck. "Come on, prince charming. Be human again so we can hit the road."

The pumpkin shimmies and hops and nearly does a backflip. I have just enough time to duck for cover before a loud *splat* echoes through the crepuscule. I peek out from above the car and see Jack standing in the carcass of a squash.

Literally.

"You okay?" I ask, rushing toward him. I run my hands down his chest where the tranquilizers would have hit him. There isn't one needle prick or one single blemish.

The man is perfect, even naked in the pre-dawn, wearing nothing by pumpkin.

All hail the king of the pumpkin patch.

"I'm fine, V. Maybe stop running your hands on me, though." He grins like it's the most appropriate time to make a dick joke.

"Get your ass in the car. We gotta make like a Jack and blow."

"Not funny," he mumbles, settling back into his seat.

"A little funny," I shoot back with a snort, starting the vehicle.

"I wonder why you turn back to your human shape. Think it has to do with the threat being gone?"

"Maybe," he answers, wincing on the hay-covered seat.

I would like to report that I'm a good little non-agent and drive the speed limit and obey all of the rules of the road once we're we *finally* spat out of the forest trail. It would be a lie and not so bold-faced because time is of the essence.

"If they found us, it means either Lisbeth managed to find my coordinates or Agent Val Downer isn't exactly on the up and up."

I ponder his words for a few moments. "Who does your gut tell you is behind the attack?"

"It's gotta be Lisbeth. She has the cash to hire muscle. Downer? Not so much. Besides, if Downer is a mole, wouldn't she report to the same people as Lisbeth, if not the woman herself?"

"Hmm. Yeah. I guess that's a fair point, but there could be *two* different groups of people after you."

Jack groans. "Great. That's all I need."

"I guess there's no sense in us trying to figure out everything right now. We're naked and in a car that is currently being tracked by FUC."

"So much for our trek through the woods." Jack is wistful as he takes my hand in his.

Do I need two hands to drive? Nope. Not if it means holding hands with Jack.

"We'll have to go with your plan, then. Drive in the opposite direction that they would expect, which would be right toward FUC and Mila's house. When we spot a town, we can ditch this SUV and—" I stop myself short.

"What? What's wrong?"

"Well, depending on which bag we were able to grab, we might not have any cash." I roll my lips into my mouth and try to take a deep breath. "I can't steal a car."

"I'll steal a car."

"You can't do that," I gasp. "It's a crime. I'm an agent of the law, and I can't actually commit an offense or let you do it for us."

"I'm pretty sure your director won't be mad in this situation."

"I mean I'm making a hash of this mission. First, I fall for my charge. Then I *sleep* with him. *Then* I proceed to go on the run nude, with no method of communication and without money."

Jack squeezes my hand, and I glance at him when it's safe to do so. The last thing I need is to kill us in a crash. "What?" I ask.

"You just said a really nice thing."

"I did?" I laugh nervously. "It sounds like I listed a whole big mess."

"You fell for your charge."

Oh. Shit. I'm naked and blushing.

It's not just my cheeks that are burning and red. My whole *body* is, and Jack can see it all. I grip the wheel tighter with my free hand and scour my brain for some kind of explanation, but I draw a blank.

"That not a bad thing, you know." He interlaces our fingers. "I should probably tell you right now... I fell for you, too."

"It's weird," I sigh.

"It is," he agrees with a smirk. "Very soon. Very quick."

"Seven days."

"Alone in a cabin, though," he amends with a shrug.

"Right. That makes a difference, does it?"

"Yes, of course," he answers.

"Are there dating rules I don't know about?"

"There might be," he teases. "The rulebook I got explained things very clearly. When you meet a woman who makes you as nuts as much as she makes you laugh, then you know it's the real deal."

"I make you nuts?"

He chuckles. "And you make me laugh."

"Well, as sweet as this is, we still shouldn't have done what we did. We should have waited until this was all over. Director Cooper won't be happy with me. More than that, if we hadn't been in the bedroom together, those goons might not have been able to get the jump on us."

"Um, not sure that could have gone better, actually. I think I scared the crap out of them when I shifted into the pumpkin thing."

"About that..." I chanced another side-eye his way. "How did *that* happen?"

"Well, you gave me the idea, actually."

For the next forty-five minutes, Jack goes into detail about the science behind the transformation. I understand the first two minutes, but the rest is way over my head. I'd need a Ph.D. in genes and botany—and maybe a few other disciplines—to understand how he managed to morph his genome.

"I'm just gonna call it magic," I tease.

"Science is kinda like magic. A potion is simply another word for experiment."

"If that were true, I would have liked my science class a lot more in high school." I tap my fingers on the well. "I didn't like those classes much. The debate team was more my speed."

"I can definitely see that. You're great on your feet."

I snort my argument. "I *always* had a strategy in the courtroom. Tonight? Not so much. I didn't have much of a plan beyond *keep us alive*."

"It worked."

"For now," I argue. "We need to get to safety."

"You're right. There's a small village down this road. We'll be able to boost a car. I'll leave a note," he quickly adds as I'm about to argue with him. "We'll make it clear that we're going to bring the car back to them eventually."

"Fine," I mumble.

But really, we don't have a choice.

We're low on options, and the sun is about to come out.

18

NORBERT

I'm not going to lie. When we finally manage to find a car to *borrow*, I'm relieved.

Not because I want us to put clothes on or anything so prudish, but I'm sitting on a pile of hay, and that shit is itchy as hell.

At the time, it seemed like a good idea to morph into some kind of scarecrow figure. Now, I am seriously doubting my decision. Maybe I should have focused on tweaking the whole blasting-open part of the shift.

If I am going to be an exploding pumpkin every time I have to turn back into my human form, I will buy stock in cleaning product companies.

The bag Vera made me grab from the house had a bunch of my clothes in it. They're too big for Vera, but that works in our favor, given her allergy. The sun is beginning to rise, and the only car we managed to find *doesn't* have tinted windows. Not to the extent that Vera needs, anyway. She's in the passenger seat, bundled up in layers to protect her skin from the rays poking through the early morning sky.

Vera directs me as we drive toward her cousin's home. If

calculations are correct, it'll be the middle of the day by the time we get there. That's the middle of the night for nocturnal creatures like Mila and Vera.

"It must be quite difficult to be nocturnal," I comment, hoping to relieve some of the mounting pressure. It's not like we're out on a jaunty drive. This isn't a laugh. We're on the run, and until we figure out who was behind the attack on my cabin, we can't really trust anyone. Instead of focusing on that and panicking—which could very well lead to me becoming a pumpkin again—I can make pleasant conversation. "Do you wish you didn't have a sun allergy?"

Vera shrugs. "It would make life easier if I could be out during the day. It made my career as a lawyer very difficult. It's not like the most upstanding citizens were up for meetings in the dead of night. I always had to sneak into the courthouse because they don't have night court. I got used to the strange schedule, but I missed the moon."

"Huh. You missed the moon?"

"Yeah. I suspect it would be like you not seeing the sun for days. You need it like I need the moon."

"That's interesting. I never even thought of that. You're a night-blooming flower."

Vera giggles. "Did you seriously compare me to a plant that grows by the light of the moon?"

"Yup. I sure did."

"Only a botanist and subsistence farmer would find that romantic."

"The question is, did *you* find it romantic, V?"

Her breath catches, and from the corner of my eye, I see her smirk.

"Yeah, but only because it comes from you."

"Fair enough."

"Jack, can I ask you something? I don't want to upset you..."

"Go right ahead. It's the perfect time. It's not like I can run away from you."

She laughs and toys with the sleeve of her shirt. "I wonder why you like to stay hidden in your cabin. You're obviously a brilliant scientist if you can create a blood alternative in such a short amount of time. Not to mention that you also managed to tweak your shifter genes *twice* now. What's that about?"

"You give me too much credit. I had most of the work already done for the shifter stuff. As soon as I realized what I'd done to myself, I started working on *not* being a defenseless gourd every time I'm threatened. The blood thing, well..." I run a hand over my mouth. "I did a lot of research and experiments when I was still working for Lisbeth. It wasn't too hard to do. I basically pulled the nutrients and added some water and flavoring. I know the Bloody Doctor's work inside out at this point. She broke down everything anyone would ever need to know about blood. That's why her work is so critical. She's unlocked quite a few mysteries. In the wrong hands, that knowledge is..."

"Dangerous?" Vera offers.

"Exactly. When I was working for Lisbeth, I asked her about the ethics of it all. If there were certain lines I wasn't to cross. She told me I had a free pass. Assured me that there wasn't a thing I could do that she couldn't protect me from. It might not cast me in the best of lights, but when you give a scientist *carte blanche*, things can get interesting. I didn't concern myself with the morality of what I was doing. I wanted to find the cure to all illnesses. Can you imagine what that would do for the world? No more disease? There would never be another pandemic. There would be no more endemics. No more cancer or degenerative diseases."

"That's pretty revolutionary."

"It would have been, yeah. But that's not what Lisbeth wanted from me. It was all about immortality. She wanted me to focus on how to regenerate cells so the body never ages and dies. That was too tall of an order for my skills."

"You did it because of your parents?"

I sigh and let my mind spin out before answering a shaky, "Yes."

"They died suddenly, and that made an impact on you."

"It did. Imagine it. I was a kid, living in the rainforest. The only people I ever interacted with were my parents and a few locals. I wasn't exactly socialized properly."

"So that's why you prefer living in your cabin alone."

"I choose when I want to be with people. I get tired very easily around others. Talking and all that is difficult."

"You seem fine around me."

"Well, that's because you're quite easy to be around, V."

"Oh."

"I mean it. When Downer first told me that I would have to host an agent for my own protection, I fully intended to make that person sleep in a tent outside. But then *you* showed up, and I don't know. I didn't get the usual panic I get. I don't know if it was because you didn't seem overly fazed about the pumpkin thing. After the Lisbeth debacle, I didn't think I could trust another human, but you walked in with your attitude and lip gloss... and your morals."

"My morals?"

"Yeah. You left your job as a lawyer because you couldn't uphold the law. Because you had to defend some bad people. You became an agent, and you were adamant that you'd report my ass to FUC and the Cryptozoian Council if I stepped a toe out of line."

"You like me because I follow the rules?"

"Among other things, yes." I take her hand and bring it to my lips to give it a quick kiss. "Even the fact that wouldn't steal a car even though we're on the run is refreshing. I need the physical boundary of a forest around me to feel secure. You have your principles as your boundaries. It's commendable."

"Not a very sexy quality."

"I beg to differ. Solid boundaries are definitely sexy."

She snorts. "You are not like other men, Jack Palomer."

"I know. I'm the Pumpkin King." I wink at her, grinning like a fool.

Vera snorts before laughing softly. "It's funny that you like that about me. That I like rules, I mean. I think I only developed that as a defense mechanism because of my blood thing."

"How do you mean?"

"Well, I always felt like a broken bat. I can't do a basic thing. A biological need I rely on to survive. It's basically a rule of nature. I thought if I followed all of life's other rules to the letter, then it wouldn't matter so much if I could drink blood or not." She shrugs, sighing. "I've been trying to make up for it my whole life. I try to perfect every other way that I can."

I tighten my grip on her hand. "So I'm a recluse because I don't know how to interact with people and I'm wary of all of the social norms, and you're hyperaware of them. We're a pair and a half."

"We really are."

"This was my way of asking you how this thing between us is gonna play, by the way."

"You're my charge, and I don't have my badge yet. Would you be mad if I want to put a pin in it until it's not against the rules anymore?"

"Sure thing, V." I kiss her hand again, but I sure hope it's not our last kiss.

19

VERA

The house Mila shares with her husband is... *normal.*

It has a yard, flowerbeds, and cute shutters. I can't exactly imagine Mila working in the garden and tending to the plants. T-Bone, now, there is another story.

This house *screams* T-Bone. I can only imagine that the inside resembles something that would make Dracula proud. It's probably some kind of compromise. Mila and T-Bone could *not* be any more different. They are polar opposites, but they fit so well together.

Not to go full cheese, but they really do complete each other.

I really hate bringing trouble to Mila so close to her due date, but if she ever found out that I was dealing with Bloody Doctor stuff and *didn't* involve her, I'd be in serious trouble.

Do not piss off a forensic anthropologist. They know how to get rid of bones.

"This is it?" Jack asks, pointing to the house.

"Yup."

He loops around the neighborhood and parks the car near a park. Leaving a stolen car in my pregnant cousin's laneway is hardly a good idea. We don't want to draw attention to our location.

Dressed in clothes that are way too big for me, I rush through the streets. It's only about a two-minute walk, but by the time I'm standing under the awning, I'm in a bit of pain.

The cure for a bad sun allergy reaction?

Blood.

No, thank you!

I knock on the door, banging against it like a lunatic. "Mila, it's Vera. Please open the door."

It swings open, and T-Bone stands there in a pair of boxers, his hair a mess of blond spikes. He rubs sleep from his face. "Vera? What's happening?"

"What in the name of anthropometers and Boley gauges is going on?" Mila wobbles over in a black nightgown with the words *Lazy Bones* printed across her baby bump.

"Can we come in?" I plead. "There's been some trouble."

T-Bone motions us forward, and we settle in a very neat, very tidy living room. For a few seconds, I think that there is no Mila influence on the decor, but I notice the painting. It's a massive piece that takes up nearly the entire wall. The canvas is white with a whole mess of inkblots à la Rorschach test splashed over it in shades of black and red. Either I'm harboring some pretty intense homicidal compulsions or the painting is actually meant to depict a few skeletons.

A little freaked, I look away, only to spot a series of skulls on the bookshelf.

And a set of teeth used as bookends.

And a few scalpels laid on red velvet encased in a shadowbox.

I wonder what T-Bone thinks of his home's decor, but he must not care. Every time he looks at Mila, his eyes burst out in tiny red hearts. The doting and loving husband helps Mila settle on the couch.

We go through the introductions, momentarily pretending that this is a normal social call. Sort of difficult thing to do when both hosts are in their pajamas and still fuzzy with sleep.

"How far along are you?" Jack asks, sitting in an armchair. He tries not to stare at the quilt patterned over with tiny skulls neatly folded on the coffee table.

"I'm a thousand years late," Mila answers while T-Bone says, "Our little one should be along in the next couple of days. They're talking about inducing if the baby isn't born by next Friday."

"I'm about to induce myself," Mila grumbles.

T settles next to her on the couch, his hand going to her thigh in a comforting squeeze. They're very different but so damn in love. It gives me hope for Jack and me, even though we're not supposed to even be together. Or even thinking about being together.

"Now, will you tell us why you're here in the middle of the day?" Mila winces and rubs her belly. "It's gonna be a boy. We've gotta a bull in here, I swear. He's got horns and loves to jab into my organs."

"If you're here, I take it to mean that your guardian duty isn't going too well." T-Bone is serious and stern with a twinge of concern.

"You're right," I agree before delving into the whole story.

Jack interjects and adds the information he can about Vitality Holdings and Lisbeth Bannon. When he gets to the Bloody Doctor's research, Mila blanches.

"Will I ever be free of that woman's actions?" She looks down at her belly. "I promise you I'll be a batshit mother, but not like that. Okay? I won't kill anyone, but I will embarrass you because it is my uterus-given right." She focuses her eyes back onto Jack. "Please tell me you didn't find the key to immortality."

"No, I didn't. But I think it's fair to assume I wasn't the only person Bannon and VH taped to look into the research." He continues the tale of our adventures up to this very moment.

"You're right. We need Jessie on this. Good thing it's daytime. She'll be up and at work." T grabs the phone, but my squeak of surprise stops him.

"We don't know who we can trust at FUC." My words are like a bomb.

Mila and T are two loyal and dedicated FUC agents.

"That's preposterous," Mila gasps. "Like a mole could ever operate under Alyce Cooper's nose."

"This is a secure line. Jessie set it up herself. This is as safe as need be," T-Bone promises.

Jack and I exchange an uneasy look.

"I just don't want to put you in any danger." I point toward Mila's stomach.

She waves me off. "If anything, the excitement will make this little creature come out. Besides, this is too important. If I'm gonna give birth, I'd rather do it in a world where my mother's research isn't going to be a long and overreaching shadow on my child. Make the call, beefcake."

T-Bone heads for the kitchen to have a rushed and hushed conversation.

"That's fair." Jack runs a hand back through his hair. "I'm really sorry I've brought this down on you."

She shakes her head. "If it wasn't you, it'd be someone else. There are a lot of psychos out there who are trying to find the secrets to immortality. Bannon and whoever she is working with are hardly the first people to take the Bloody

Doctor's work to heart. Unfortunately, they won't be the last."

"It would be nice if they were, though," I comment.

"Jessie is on the case," T-Bone announces. "She'll stay at FUCN'A to not arouse any suspicion, but she's looking into Bannon and VH. She'll call as soon as there's news. She'll also look into Val Downer and FUCN'A's Cryptozoian Council rep, Erhart Knope, to see if there are any links between them and VH."

"And what can we do right now?" I ask. "I could bring Jack to another location. Someplace safe."

"Not a chance," Mila roars. "He stays right here where we can keep an eye on him. If this goes bad, I'd rather T be around to help you out. Last time, they came at you with tranquilizers. Your whole pumpkin-scarecrow thing scared them once, but now that they know what you can do, you've lost the element of surprise. They'll come with more effective weapons next time, and probably with more people."

"She's right," T-Bone agreed. "You're to stay here. I've got a small arsenal of weapons in the basement, anyway."

"But we can hardly shift to defend ourselves in the heart of suburbia."

"Why not? T shifted last Halloween. We had a whole demonic farm theme going."

"Hardly the same thing," I point out to my eccentric cousin.

"We really have to... wait here until something happens?" Jack isn't too pleased with this plan.

"That's exactly right," T says. "Until we have more intel from Jessie, there is nothing we can do. We can't pick a fight with an enemy we don't know."

"I feel useless," Jack grumbles. "And a right ass for bringing this to your door."

"Stop," Mila grunts as she tries to stand up. "I need something to eat. I'm ravenous. Let's take this meeting to the kitchen. Might as well graze and talk while we wait for our next step."

T-Bone and Mila retreat to the kitchen, but I hang back in the living room with Jack. "We can't do anything more right now than wait until we have more information. I know you don't like this, but there's nothing we can do. You're still an important witness in all of this. As an almost FUC agent, my job is to keep you safe and out of harm's way. It's the same for T-Bone and Mila."

"I don't like that I caused more trouble instead of making the world better."

"Well, when all of this is resolved, I'm sure you'll find a way to make amends if that's how you feel."

Jack nods, but his eyes have lost their spark.

He feels really bad. It's written all over his face.

I can only hope that he doesn't use this as an excuse to continue his reclusive ways.

I can't exactly date a man who won't leave his forest.

20

NORBERT

When I'm in the lab, waiting to see how one experiment or another works out, I keep busy. I've typically got a few things going on all at once to make sure that my time doesn't lapse into quiet and motionless moments.

Being a subsistence farmer on top of that is also helpful.

If I don't take care of my crops, I don't eat.

There's a mound of food on the kitchen table in front of me, so that's *that* need taken care of. There *really* is nothing for me to do but sit here and speculate.

And think.

Lots and lots of thinking.

I'm about ready to rip my hair out at the roots. Vera's hand hasn't left my thigh since we sat down thirty minutes ago. She can feel my impatience and the urgency burning a hole through my sanity. She gives me a whole bouquet of encouraging nudges and smiles.

Mila hovers her laptop on her baby bump as she scrolls through gossip columns and social media feeds, looking for any mention of Lisbeth Bannon. Apparently, you can't be the CEO of a large corporation without making some headlines every now and again. Mila and T-Bone aren't too concerned about having their research ping any VH security alerts because of the VPN, firewalls, and all of this other security stuff Jessie, the computer pro, set them up with.

Whoever this Jessie woman is, I need to get her help to secure the cabin, apparently.

If I can ever go back.

"Lisbeth Bannon dated Jefferson Cabot?" Mila scrunches up her face and turns the device to show us a picture of Bannon with one of Hollywood's heartthrobs. The guy is in everything, and it's not because he's got talent. "Isn't he a groundhog shifter? Rich, connected daddy?" *That's* why he's in everything.

"He is," Vera answers. "He's basically shifter royalty. His dad is a big deal in the finance world. I remember reading an article about it. Daddy Dearest was really pissed his son didn't want to follow in his footsteps and went into acting instead."

"So we have a rich and famous actor with a tie to the finance world who just happens to be a shifter." I sigh and run my hands back through my hair, hoping to renew blood flow and get a new idea or lead from thin air.

"That can't be a coincidence." Mila continues to scroll. "What if Bannon is out there, dating all these dudes she thinks can help her cause?"

"Mila," T warns before shooting me an apologetic glance.

"What?" She shrugs. "Sorry, that was hurtful, Jack."

"No need to apologize. You're not wrong. She used me. Stands to reason she would do the same thing to another dude out there."

"Oh!" Mila gasps. "Jessie is trying to video chat. Hey, lady. Did you already find something?"

Jessie clicks her tongue. "Some*thing*? Try things. Lots and lots of *things*."

"Gather round, kids." Mila lays the computer on the table where we can all see Jessie's face on the screen. We do another quick round of introductions, but it's pretty clear that Jessie is burning to tell us something.

"You lot need to be super careful. I did some digging into Vitality Holdings and lemme tell you. None of it is good. From what I can tell using *purely* legal ways"—the flush on her cheeks suggests otherwise—"there's a bunch of rich and powerful shifters out there who don't feel like our shifter nature is enough. They want immortality."

"We know this." Mila snaps her fingers. "If anyone tells me I'm being impatient, I'll ask you to refer back to the Hairy Coo growing inside me who is two days away from his or her due date."

"Right." Jessie grins. "I'll try not to take it personally. Now, these bad shifter types are *funding* VH. From what I was able to find in such a short amount of time is that Vitality is nothing but a big front. Yep. You heard me right. One of the largest beauty companies in the world is actually this massive conspiracy to take over the world."

"No one is surprised by this." Vera rolls her eyes. "I'm addicted to my cotton candy lip gloss, but I hate that I feel the need to cover my whole face in concealer to hide a single zit."

"Preach," Mila quips. "D'you know people are *already* asking me how I plan to bounce back and get my pre-baby body? Fucking ridiculous. It'll be what it'll be. I grew a human. What did those fuckers do today?"

"My hero," T-Bone says before kissing the top of her head. He means it, too.

There isn't one ounce of sarcasm in his voice. The man is

completely in awe of his partner. Mila and T remind me of my parents. Both strong in their own right and in their own beliefs but so perfectly accepting of the other's strengths. It's something to see.

I long for that.

I never really let myself believe I wanted it, but now that I'm surrounded by people and a couple very much in love, I've realized something.

The reason why I always need to be busy at the cabin is that I'm lonely.

Deeply, profoundly lonely.

If I keep working and occupy every single waking hour with one dire task or another, then the solitude can't get to me. I'm above it somehow.

How will I be able to go back to it now that I've discovered the meaning behind it?

Do I even *want* to go back to it?

If I survive this whole ordeal, what do I want my life to look like? Alone in a cabin off in the wilderness?

No. That's not what I want anymore.

I'd like a house not too different from this one—okay, maybe a lot different where aesthetics are concerned. Maybe a partner to share my life with...

Perhaps a woman with a hazel gaze and pretty brown hair that always smells like cotton candy and happiness.

"Are you with us, Jack?" Mila pulls me out of my tailspin.

Every pair of eyes is on me, including Jessie's. "Sorry, what? Did I miss something?"

"We need to know where you met Lisbeth," Vera repeats. "Where you worked when you weren't in your lab. Where she lived. Her usual haunts. It'll give us a clue as to who she's working for."

"Can't you track down the off-shore accounts?" I aim my question to Jessie.

She laughs like it's the most hilarious thing in the world. "Oh, sure. Because they're not smart enough to hide behind more companies with more fronts than a Dungeons and Dragons' dice. It would take me a long time to pull at that thread. Time we might not have if they're after you."

"And let's be real," T cuts in. "If they only wanted to kidnap you or silence you *before* they knew what you could do? That'll be nothing compared to their excitement when they realize you've turned yourself into an invulnerable *pumpkin*."

"I'm not even going to ask," Jessie quips from the monitor. "On paper, VH is only the larger corporation behind all of Vitality's products and smaller companies. But no one who is on the up and up has *this* long of a trail."

"What's our next step then?" Vera wonders. "Why does it feel like we'll have to bring Director Cooper in for this?"

"Because we have to," Mila answers. "Not only is she our boss but if Erhart Knope and the Cryptozoian Council have gone rogue or have a mole, she needs to know."

"There isn't a chance in hell Erhart Knope is a bad guy. He's is more straight edge than T." Jessie quickly adds, "Sorry, T."

"You're not wrong." He shrugs.

"Are you really telling me that we have to tell our boss that I fucked up my first non-mission? Leaving the cabin? Stealing a car?" Vera puts her hand over her mouth. "I think I'm gonna pass out from the disappointed look on her face and she's not even here yet."

"Not gonna lie. Alyce will be hella pissed at you. But you also made some very good calls. Don't freak out just yet. Let's see where this all leads, okay? You'll be fine, Vera. And we're right here with you."

"See?" T-Bone says. "My wife is gonna be the best damn mom."

Mila clicks her tongue, but she's also pleased. "Easy, beefcake." She blows him a kiss before passing the landline over to Vera. "It's secure. Promise. Call Alyce."

Vera nods and heaves out a breath before calling her boss to admit she might very well have fucked up her career as an agent before it even got started.

21

VERA

Director Alyce Cooper is not the kind of woman you want to piss off.

She is a—*the*—boss for a reason.

I also admire her. A lot.

Letting her down after what happened at the graduation is a little too much for me. As soon as I end the call—after Director Cooper coolly told me she was on her way and that we *would discuss it in person*—I have to rush to the bathroom to splash cold water on my face and neck.

Rule breaking isn't something I'm exactly used to. Disappointing figures of authority I admire? That's a big bucket of mental flagellation.

The gentle sound of knocking pulls me away from my racing thoughts.

"V, it's Jack. Wanna talk?"

I slowly open the door and lean against the frame. Jack mimics my position, his head hovering inches over mine. His lips graze my temple while his hands grip my hips.

"I'd ask if you're okay, but I can tell you're freaking out."

"I broke so many rules."

"Sometimes, to do the right thing, you gotta do a couple bad things. From where I'm standing, you did nothing wrong. You kept me alive and brought me to a safe place."

"But then there's the other thing…"

"I definitely don't think that was wrong. In fact, I think that was really good. Fantastic, even. I'm looking forward to more of that." He smiles at me. "Are there really rules that prevent relationships between agent and charge?"

"I assume there have to be. It's a weird power dynamic, isn't it?"

"I gladly relinquish all of my power to you, oh my batty queen." He winks and pulls me into his arms for a hug so warm, so powerful, that even my soul feels it.

"All your power, huh?" I tease before inhaling his sweet woodsy scent. It's as comforting as it's emboldening.

"I actually have a lot of faith that this will all work out for the best."

"Oh, really? How's that?"

"Just a feeling I have, but I can't see Director Cooper being mad that you did the best you could in an impossible situation. And if she is mad? We'll deal with whatever comes. Together."

"Together," I repeat, as if the word were foreign to me. It's not, but the idea of Jack and me as a unit, a team, for an extended time is a potent thought. Almost as much as the man himself.

Holding hands—because Mila will hardly rat me out to our boss—we make our way to the living room. My cousin is in the large armchair, feet up, eyes closed, and hands rubbing her belly. She peeks at us and grins.

"So that's how it is. I told T something was going between you two. Tell me everything."

"Mila, leave them be. Rest, Spooky. You need to rest."

"I know, I know. Apparently, I'm supposed to stock up on sleep before the baby is born. As if it works that way. *Exhausted?* No, thanks. I'm good. I had a wee nap before pushing a twenty-pound coo out my—" She clicks her tongue. "I'm a tad scared about giving birth."

"You don't say," I tease. "You're literally the strongest, most stubborn woman I know. You'll be fine."

"I second that sentiment," T-Bone cuts in.

"Besides, you know I'll desperately want some baby cuddles. You two can nap during that time." I mean it, too. I hope Mila knows that. It's not like she has a doting mother around to help her with her fears about motherhood.

Aunt Sveta is in prison for hundreds of years because she killed over three hundred people. That doesn't exactly scream, *Let's go spend some time with Granny.*

The energy in the house is tense as we wait for Director Cooper, but there is every chance that it's only my own panic coloring my perception.

When the doorbell rings—interrupting a very heated debate between T-Bone and Jack about the right kind of grazing grass for cattle—I jump to my feet and rush for the door.

"Director Cooper, thanks so much for coming," I say as I let her into the house.

She walks in with all of the gravitas that is attached to her title. I want to duck tail and run like a kid that's thrown a baseball through the window. I'm not a child, though. I'm a grown woman who has to face the consequences of her actions.

"You gonna tell me what the hell is going on?" she demands, crossing her arms.

"Well..." I stumble over my tongue.

"Out with it, Vera." She snaps her fingers at me before

going toward the living room. She greets the others with a curt head nod, still waiting for me to speak.

"See..." I begin as I nervously shuffle from one foot to the other. "Everything was going fine until three intruders attacked us." I go into detail, telling my boss everything that's happened in the last twenty-four hours.

Only *not* everything. I don't tell her anything about Jack and me. Not yet. Let's take things one at a time.

Mila and T-Bone jump in, filling in the director with Jessie's findings. She doesn't seem overly concerned that we went to the tech guru before going to the boss. In fact, she leans back in her seat and listens to the whole sordid tale as if she were watching her favorite soaps. It's not exactly too far off the mark.

Stranger than fiction and all that.

She doesn't even bat an eye when we tell her about Jack and his pumpkin situation.

"You should hear some of the stuff that's out there in the world. I'm pretty sure nothing can faze me anymore. I think my last shock came when this one got married." She hooks a thumb toward Mila, but there's humor in her tone. She's joking with her employee.

This gives me hope that she won't be too pissed off that I slept with a charge. After all, T and Mila met on a case. Sure, they were both agents, but Director Alyce Cooper has to know that sometimes life just happens.

Once all is said and done, Jack jumps in. "Is it possible that Val Downer is a mole? What about Erhart Knope? If it's not FUC, then it has to be one of them," Jack insists. "There's a chance it could be Lisbeth, but she never knew where I lived."

"And you didn't think it was weird that the woman you were screwing didn't care where you lived?" Director Cooper pulls no punches, but I don't really want to hear his response.

By the flushed color of his cheeks, Jack doesn't want to reply. "I made it clear that I like my privacy and that I didn't have a conventional address. She didn't question it, and I like my solitude."

"That's weird, but it's your life." Director Cooper shrugs. "Let's put Lisbeth aside for a moment. There isn't a chance in hell that Erhart Knope is crooked. He's way too sanctimonious for that. But if there is a chance one of his people is more bent than a stop sign in a hurricane, I want to be the one to tell him."

"They have a contentious relationship," Mila explains.

"That hyena shifter *loves* to lord it over me that he's the rep for the Cryptozoian Council. Like he's better than me. My *superior*. Pfft. I am the Director of the FUCN'A, for fuck's sake. All new agents pass through my doors. That means something." She purses her lips. "Did Jessie find anything about this Val Downer? Koala shifter, isn't she?"

"Yes," Jack answers. "We have no more information than that. We were waiting on you to make any sort of further decision."

"That's a good idea. Now I get to call Erhart Knope and give him this news." The woman rubs her hands together, relishing the thought of one-upping Knope. "If this turns out to be the mole, I'm gonna be so happy. I'll buy you fresh hay for your scarecrow. Now, someone give me the phone. It's time to break Erhart's heart."

22

NORBERT

I am a nervous wreck.

I can't stop fidgeting, and apparently, that's a dead give-away that I'm up to something, so I really need to quit it. The problem is I can't. Not only am I more than a little anxious about what is moments away from going down but I'm also concerned that I'll gourd out before anything can happen.

Not good.

Actually, pretty fucking bad. Not only for me but for Vera and all of FUC and the Cryptozoian Council.

After goading Erhart Knope for a good ten minutes, Director Cooper explained to him that he might have a mole in his organization. We decided that if Lisbeth was involved, it had to mean she somehow got to Val Downer.

For a whopping fifteen minutes, Erhart Knope refused to believe that one of the council members was responsible, but the more Director Cooper explained things to him, the quieter he got.

He helped us set this whole sting operation.

Erhart Knope is helping us catch Val Downer.

To say that the hyena shifter is angry is a bit of an under-statement. Sort of like stating blood doesn't agree with Vera.

Vera and I are standing by an armored car in a community park parking lot, patiently waiting for Downer. The trap is set, and all we have to do is wait and see what happens.

"Are you okay?" Vera asks.

"Yes," I lie. "You?"

"Yes," she lies right back to me. "Not in the least bit nervous."

I know that T-Bone is close by with a whole team of agents. Mila wanted to come, but we had to put our foot down. We couldn't bring a very pregnant woman who can't shift to a dangerous setup. She was pissed. She feels as responsible as me because this was all linked to her mother's research.

I brought it all back to her doorstep days before she gives birth to her first child. That doesn't make me feel too great. I'll babysit their bundle of joy as much as they allow me. A small apology token.

Who knows, maybe Vera will be with me. Good practice for when we have our own batty pumpkin.

Really, Jack. So not the time.

A black car pulls in beside ours about three minutes later than scheduled.

My gut tightens, and I clench my jaw down to keep from shouting and raging at the agent who put lives in danger. And for what? I don't know her motivation yet, and I'm not too sure it matters.

Immortality is a dumb thing to chase. This coming from the guy who brought Lisbeth Bannon and her cronies *that* much closer.

"You had me worried, Norbert." Val slams her car door.

"I've been trying to call the satellite phone nonstop. I was scared something happened."

"Something did happen," I shoot back.

Here it is. The moment of truth.

Or not. Rather, the moment that decides how good of a liar I am.

"I was going over the files you asked me to double-check. I found something. Another file. One that's…" I swallow and look over to Vera. Her face is an unreadable mask. She is a force. So damn strong. I let her strength and resolve sink into me. "The file I have on this changes everything." I hold up a memory stick. It's shaped like a bone because it belongs to Mila.

Val's eyes light up, and she steps forward, her hand held out expectantly. "That's wonderful. It'll bet it's what we need."

She leaves her statement open-ended because she thinks I'm thinking about the trial.

She has no idea I know exactly what she's talking about.

The key to immortality.

At least, that's the hope. Before we get the rest of the agents to move in on her, Vera and I have to try to get her to talk.

"You should call Erhart Knope right away to let him know," Vera says, holding out a phone.

Downer's face falls. "No. I'd rather deliver this news in person."

"I insist," Vera presses, wagging the phone.

The other woman rolls her eyes. "And why should I take my cues from you? You haven't even fully graduated yet."

Vera grins. "Matter of time. I can call him myself."

"Fine."

Downer pulls her own device from her pant pockets and puts on a great big show of calling her boss.

"Hey, Knope. For whatever reason, FUC pseudo-agent Vera insisted on calling you to let you know we might have the evidence we need to charge VH with a lot more than toxic waste dumping." She pauses and gives us the thumbs-up as if she is listening intently to Erhart.

We know she can't be talking to him. It's simply not possible.

She continues her fake conversation for some of the most awkward seconds of my life.

It's one thing to watch someone lie, but to witness them lying so badly and with such conviction? It makes my skin crawl. I'm embarrassed for her and for what is about to happen.

"Not sure why you absolutely needed me to do that, but there. It's done. Happy?" Her anger is barely contained.

"You could do with some acting classes." Vera holds up the phone.

Only, it's not hers. The device belongs to Erhart Knope. The man Val Downer *supposedly* called.

That was the beauty of the trap.

Had the phone rang in Vera's hand, we would have explained everything to her and apologized for not trusting her.

Now, we had her dead to rights.

"I don't understand." Downer keeps cool, but there is a hint of fear in her voice.

"This is Erhart's phone. You know, the guy my boss reports to, who in turn reports our movements to *your* boss. Or your *Cryptozoian Council* boss, I should say, not whoever you're working for on the side. You know, the people to whom you've been feeding classified FUC and Cryptozoian

Council info." Vera blinks those beautiful long lashes of hers, daring Downer to contradict her.

"I don't know what you're playing, but this isn't funny." She takes a step back, edging toward her car.

"You should know..." Vera points toward the play structure and the group of people playing baseball on the field. "Everyone you see there? They're agents. Erhart is over there with Director Cooper and more agents. You're caught, Val."

The koala shifter's eyes go wide, her jaw slack. "You're lying."

"No," Vera assures her. "You're in a lot of trouble. The only way you can lessen the hurt that's coming your way is to tell us who you're working for."

"You've lost your mind. I can't tell you *anything*. They'll kill me. They said if I didn't help, they would kill me. They injected me with some kind of serum. If I don't get an antidote every day, I die. They send it every evening to make sure I've cooperated throughout the day."

Vera and I exchange a glance. This turn of events is definitely probable. It sure sounds like something Lisbeth would do, but it's also the perfect cover.

I need the bad guys because only they can save me.

We need to push a bit more.

"You could've told your superiors," Vera points out.

Downer scoffs. "Would you? You've been on *one* mission. I bet you've already broken a rule or two. It's not that cut and dry. I can't *die*. I've got a family."

Vera considers a moment. "Well, lucky for you, you've got the best at FUC. You know that. I'm sure they'll do what they can to help you if you're honest with us. Who are you working for?"

"Zeus and Hera."

I snort. "Come off it."

Downer throws her phone at me. Momentarily distracted, I grab for the device while she makes a run for her car. Vera, quick on her feet, and one hell of an agent, is ready for her. She leaps forward, pins Downer to the car, and holds her in place.

"Get off. Let me go." Downer squirms and tries to wiggle out of the hold.

Vera sighs. "Not a chance. We were having a really nice chat. You were telling us about Zeus and Hera. Go on."

"They'll kill me."

"Yeah, you said that. Your boss and peers just saw you trying to evade, so maybe you should be more concerned that now the good guys won't want to help you. Beware the hand that feeds you lies or something like that."

"That's not even the saying. You're a dumb newbie who doesn't have a badge. You don't have the authority to do this."

"No," Vera agrees. "But they do."

Downer raises her head, and off in the distance, Erhart Knope, Director Cooper, and T-Bone, accompanied by a small army of agents, stalk forward. Downer's legs buckle, and the only thing keeping her up is Vera. The agent weeps, pleading in a nonsensical way. I can't tell if she wants our help or wants to be released to her homicidal blackmailers.

"I'm done for," she whispers finally. "Please don't let me die."

"Then help us," I say with my best stern voice.

It takes her a few seconds, but when she sees the look of complete disappointment on Erhart's face, she turns toward me.

"Password for my phone is 8888. You'll see. Zeus and Hera call the shots. I've never seen them in person."

"Then how did they manage to stick you with that nasty

formula?" Vera loosens her hold on Downer as T-Bone cuffs the mole.

"They sent someone who gave me that phone," was the reply. "The guy injected me with the stuff, and then I had a call from both of them."

"Zeus and Hera?" I type in the passcode and immediately spot text conversations giving Downer all kinds of instructions, all having to do with me and the Bloody Doctor research.

"Yeah. I don't know who they are."

Vera and I hook gazes. "Lisbeth Bannon," she mouths.

I shrug. I've got no idea. Either Lisbeth has the exact same phone with the exact same deal with Zeus and Hera, or she *is* Hera.

"This is the first big lead we've got to find out who is behind VH," Vera whispers to me as we watch Downer being hauled away. "We need to get this phone to Jessie right away."

"This isn't over," I sigh, dejected and disappointed.

"No," Vera responds honestly as she takes my hand in hers. "But we're one step closer."

"Vera," Director Cooper shouts.

She gives me a sad smile and goes off with her boss. Being the badass agent I know she will be.

Hell, that she already *is*.

23

VERA

This is it.

This is my big moment.

And this time, there will be no paper cut and no passing out.

Nope.

This time, when I walk out of here, I will be a full FUC agent with a badge and everything.

"I've got to admit"—Director Cooper drums her fingers on her desk—"I'm impressed. I sent you out to keep an eye on Jack because I thought it would be easy and maybe it would rekindle your love for the law. I made a grave mistake in judgment. You were never a lawyer. You were born to be an agent. That was some good work, *Agent* Slaski."

"Thank you, Director Cooper. I just wish we had more information. Actual closure on the case."

"Me too, but we have a solid lead with this whole Zeus and Hera business. We'll find out who Lisbeth Bannon is working for. We'll uncover everyone behind Vitality Holdings. It's only a matter of time."

"I really hope so."

"That brings me to your next assignment."

My ears perk up, and I sit straight and at the ready. Director Cooper notices and gives a sly smirk.

"I enjoy your eagerness, Vera. It's commendable. Erhart Knope and I have agreed on something. Probably the first and last time that's ever gonna happen. We're starting an immortality chasers task force. A few of our senior agents will head it up, namely T-Bone. He's got good contacts with human police forces, and he also understands the desperation some of these lunatics go to, given that his mother-in-law is the Bloody Doctor. He'll do it all on base here, of course. I wouldn't take that man away from his newborn for too long."

I grin because ever since Bettina was born three days ago, T-Bone has barely set her down. He coos over his little girl, and it's quite possibly the cutest thing I've ever seen.

"I think that Mila will be happy about that, too," I comment. Delivery wasn't exactly easy, and she needs some rest.

"You're not wrong. You'll be part of this task force, but given that you're still a new agent, we're giving you something right in your wheelhouse. You'll be tailing Lisbeth Bannon. Your bat is tiny, perfect for some recon. You up for it?"

Am I up to get some dirt on the woman who used my boyfriend?

"Yes," I respond. "Absolutely."

"Great. That's what I like to hear. Now, here's what you've been waiting for." Director Cooper slides a badge over the desk and taps it. "I know you'll do me proud, Agent Slaski. And just think. You didn't even have to drink blood to get to where you are. Now get out of here. I've got a mountain of paperwork, and there's an army of people out there who want to congratulate you."

"The blindfold is hardly necessary," I grumble to Jack. "I'm a bat. I can echolocate with the best of 'em."

"Don't cheat!"

"You know I can *hear* the elevator dings, right? I know we're going to the subbasement."

"Hush now. Don't ruin the surprise," he whispers in my ear.

We exit the elevator, Jack holding on to my hand to guide me through the labyrinth that leads to Mila's office. She's on maternity leave, so I don't know why we're going to her lab or why I need to be deprived of my sight.

Jack is now a freelance scientist working in conjunction with FUC and the Cryptozoian Council, and I'm not sure how he got his hands on the key cards that access the bowels of FUCN'A.

Must be special permission or something.

A door opens and closes behind us. The whispered sounds of *sh* tickle my ears. Jack pulls at my blindfold. It falls and reveals my parents, sister, Mila, and T-Bone holding Bettina.

"Surprise," they shouted in unison, using a lower decibel as to not wake the baby.

I half expected Bettina to be born with firetruck-red hair like Mila, but that's not possible. No one—not even Mila— knows what Mila's real hair color is anymore. Bettina is blonde, probably like T. She is the cutest little pink squirming baby I've ever seen. I'll definitely be getting a whiff of her baby scent when I steal her away for a snuggle later.

"What's all this?" I ask.

"We wanted to congratulate you," Mom answers. "An agent! You did it, Vera. We're so proud of you."

"And you basically got Alyce and Erhart to start a task force. That's amazing, Vera," Mila gushes. "I'm damn proud to be your family *and* a bat."

"So damn proud," Raya says, one brow arched. "Of course you had to be a superstar here."

"Aw, thanks. You'll be one, too. I *know* it."

Raya waves me off as Dad gives me a hug. "Nice going, sweetie."

"There's cake," T-Bone announces. "Miranda made it special, just for you."

"That's sweet of her." My eyes prickle with happy tears. "You know that none of this would have been possible without Jack, right?"

The man in question drapes his arm across my shoulders and kisses my cheek. "I refuse to take any credit. You got my pumpkin butt out of the forest. In more ways than one."

Jack is keeping the cabin in the forest, but he's moving closer to FUCN'A. He still insists on being a subsistence farmer, and he's about to close on a tiny hobby farm, but he is rejoining the world in a very big way. He's still pretty shaken that his work is in the wrong hands, but he's working hard to fix that.

He even managed to perfect my blood substitute *and* create a serum that is keeping Val Downer alive.

The agent turned prisoner hasn't said much, but she doesn't *know* much. She's every bit the puppet Jack was. It's scary to think that these mysterious Zeus and Hera figures could have many people on their roster of minions.

I won't worry about that today. FUC is on the case, and that means it *will* be solved.

The silver lining is that I am an agent, I have my next assignment, and now that Jack will live closer, we can actually date.

We also never broke any rules. That makes me very happy.

We're free and clear to date.

And date we do.

Jack slept over every night this week. Maybe some relationship gurus would advise against it, insist that it isn't a good idea, but I don't care. We got to know each other while cohabitating in the smallest cabin known to man. We're used to sharing our space now.

Besides, I dare any woman to share a bed with a man like Jack and not want him there forever.

Impossible.

"You look really happy, V," he whispers in my ear, wrapping his arms around my waist.

"I am. I really am. This is one of those instances in life where you can *feel* just how right everything is. It's a happily-until-next-time sort of moments."

"Happily-until-next-time?"

"Well, yeah. We're really young and only beginning our lives together. We'll have loads of other moments like this. Soak it in, Pumpkin King. This is how *humans* grow in the pumpkin patch of life."

"I'll be there every step of the way, V. As long as you'll have me with my exploding gourd and straw and all."

"Wouldn't have it any other way, Jack."

He kisses me softly and holds me close before my family joins us by the cake.

The big bad might still be out there, but so long as we're together, lean on each other, and lead with kindness, we're winning.

EPILOGUE
RAYA

They say that comparison is a real joy killer.

I don't agree. I'd say that it doesn't so much kill joy as much as it destroys relationships.

Do I love my big sister? Yes, of course I do.

Vera helped me learn how to read. She gave me the best tricks to do hard math. She never complained when I stole her makeup or clothes. She didn't rat me out *once* when we were teens and I snuck out of the house.

Vera is loyal, kind, sweet, and so damn intelligent.

She's got it all. The whole package.

Being her little sister is *way* hard.

Vera excels at absolutely *everything* she does. She is always the smartest, the fastest. She is more clever than Rumpelstiltskin, more cunning than the Evil Queen, craftier than a genie.

The evidence?

Vera wasn't even a full agent. She'd been sent on a guardian duty, and my perfect sister managed to unearth a huge conspiracy.

Because *of* course Perfect Vera was able to sniff out a

major plot in the middle of the wilderness in a small cabin with no running electricity and limited internet access.

Her discovery prompted Director Cooper to start a task force to root out all the big players out there who are questing for immortality.

Not even a FUC agent yet and Vera is already setting the bar way too high for me—and that's saying something, seeing as I'm a bat shifter. I should be able to fly right over any goal post.

Now, I have to adjust my objectives and try to live up to the impossible standards Vera set.

The chances that I also manage to suss out a big scheme?

None.

Because not only has my big sister inspired the creation of a FUC task force but *I'm on it*

That's right.

My first assignment as a FUC agent is in the immortality chasers task force.

I can't mess it up.

I'd like to say it'll be as easy as pie to succeed, but that will be a tall order.

My mission doesn't just involve the rich and powerful shifters of the world hunting for immortality.

Nope. That would be too easy.

My assignment involves Santa Claus and a reindeer.

Sweet suffering mammal, but am I ever in for it.

The End

Or is it? Don't miss Raya Slaski's mission, *Bat and the Blitz,* coming December 2021!

And there are more FUC Academy books from other
authors coming your way soon!

To find out more about these books and more, visit worlds.EveLanglais.com or sign up for
the EveL Worlds newsletter. If you haven't already downloaded the **free Academy intro**
(written by Eve Langlais) make sure you grab it at
worlds.evelanglais.com/wordpress/book/fucacademy1!

BAT AND THE BONE

This bat likes a good bone...

Mila is a vampire bat who studies bones. She loves her steak raw but her Highland cattle shifter detectives hot.

Detective T-Bone—a tall wall of muscular man cake—arrives at FUCN'A with bad news. The Bloody Doctor is on the loose, and he needs Mila's encyclopedic knowledge on the notorious serial killer's crimes before bodies start to pile up again.

But Mila has a secret. Her obsession stems from the fact that she's the daughter trying to make up for the sins of the mother.

Will T-Bone believe that Mila's genetic link won't stop her from bringing her mother to justice? Or will he find the proof is in the blood...

Out now on all platforms!

BAT AND THE BLITZ

It's a batty world in the winter...

Raya is a bat shifter who grew up in the shadow of her perfect sibling, but she's determined to shine in her own moonlight when she becomes a FUCN'A agent. Unfortunately, her first assignment is on a task force run by her sister, and she's paired up with a grumpy—albeit ridiculously sexy—Christmas-hating reindeer.

She'd rather suck on menthol-flavoured gumdrops than take the case, but there's no other choice. She'll have to travel to Christmas Town to thwart would-be immortality chasers with a man who has a candy cane to pick with the big man in red.

The entire future of holiday magic hinges on a reindeer with no Christmas cheer, a vampire bat trying to prove herself, and a town full of secrets...

Coming December 7, 2021

ABOUT THE AUTHOR

A. Gregory writes magically delicious stories that will transport you to the places where things go bump in the night. Sometimes there's magic, other times there are shifters, but there is always a happily ever after.

instagram.com/a.gregory.paranormal